THE BOY
NEXT DOOR

THE BOY
NEXT DOOR

•

Mary Anne Taylor

AVALON BOOKS
NEW YORK

F
Tay
c. 1

PRINTED IN THE UNITED STATES OF AMERICA
ON ACID-FREE PAPER
BY HADDON CRAFTSMEN, BLOOMSBURG, PENNSYLVANIA

To Jack
For your unconditional love
and unwavering encouragement, inspiration, and faith

Chapter One

"**M**om! Where are you, Mom?" The front door slammed, and a staccato of rapid footsteps sounded across the tile floor of the foyer.

"I'm in the sun room, Jonathan." Samantha pulled her gaze from the "condominiums for rent" column in the newspaper just as her six-year-old son burst into the room.

"Can I go to the park with Trevor and Brad? We want to play softball."

"With Trevor and who?"

"Brad," a mature, masculine voice repeated, and then his large form filled the doorway. He grinned at her. "Hello, Samantha. Remember me?"

She gazed up into gold-flecked, hazel eyes as the sunlight glanced off his dark brown hair. Even after all these years, she'd have known that smile anywhere.

Pushing the newspaper aside, she rose from the

sofa. "Brad Davis. How are you? I heard that you'd moved back to Glen Arbor."

He nodded. "Several years ago. I'm doing my residency at University Hospital here. Almost finished." He wore shorts, a gray T-shirt with "Michigan University" emblazoned across the front, and sneakers without socks.

His gaze held hers. "I understand you've come back to stay for a while too."

"Yes, we arrived about a week ago." She brushed self-consciously at a strand of hair that had freed itself from the tie at the nape of her neck. "We're staying with my father until we can find a place of our own."

"Can I go, Mom? Brad's going to pitch us some balls so we can practice our batting." Jonathan jumped up and down with excitement, his blond hair bobbing over his forehead, just short of the animated blue eyes.

"Yes. Sure, you can go." Samantha smiled at his enthusiasm, then shoved her hands into the back pockets of her jeans. "It's nice of you to take them, Brad. I didn't think residents had time for this sort of thing."

"Not very often, I admit. Got lucky today." He winked at Jonathan, who turned and headed for the front door.

"I'll wait out in the car with Trevor."

"Sure, sport. I'll be there in a few minutes."

Brad's gaze returned to Samantha, and his smile faded. "I was sorry to hear about your husband's death."

A wave of the old sadness washed over her. "Thank you."

"Your Dad said it was his heart. Mid-thirties, that's awfully young."

"It was a congenital defect. We had no idea until it happened. It . . . was a shock."

"I can imagine."

The compassion in his eyes made her uncomfortable and she shifted, folding her arms across her middle. "It's been almost two years now, and I decided it was time to come home. Thought some male influence would be good for Jonathan." She gave a wan smile. "But Dad's still busy as ever."

Boyish yips sounded from the front yard, and Brad glanced in that direction. "Guess I'd better get out there."

Samantha accompanied him to the front door and then down the walkway to his dark green SUV, which stood at the curb. Trevor and Jonathan, who had been romping on the front lawn, piled into the back seat.

Brad paused before getting into the vehicle himself. "Do you plan to look for a job here? You're a nurse now, right?"

She nodded. "I'm hoping to find something in a doctor's office. The hours would be better than at the hospital, and I want to be free to spend evenings and weekends with Jonathan."

His forehead creased in thought. "I think a couple of the offices at University Hospital are looking for nurses."

She nodded again. "I have an interview with a Dr. Dwyer there tomorrow, and I'm working on another."

"Dwyer? Sure, I know him well. Nice guy." Brad grinned. "I guess I'll see you around then."

"That'd be nice."

Brad continued to gaze down at her and shifted his stance, but didn't move to get into the car.

"It's getting hot in here, Uncle Brad!"

"Yeah. Coming." He turned from Samantha with seeming reluctance and climbed in. Once inside, his eyes met hers again. "We'll only be gone about an hour."

"That's fine. Bye, guys." She stepped away from the car and lifted a hand in farewell. "Have fun at the park."

Brad started the engine and pulled slowly away from the curb. As he did so, his gaze shifted to the rearview mirror, and he watched as the distance slowly obscured the details of Samantha's features.

Lord, she was a looker! That long blond hair and fresh flawless complexion. She'd always been a cute kid, but she'd matured into an absolute beauty.

His thoughts drifted back to their younger years. They'd grown up next door to one another, and she was a good friend of his sister, Cindy. He smiled at the recollection of the two little tomboys—four years his junior—who used to pester the bejabbers out of him and his friends. Later he'd gone away to college and then medical school, and by the time he'd returned to a residency here at Michigan University, Samantha had moved to the east coast and gotten married.

But, widowed now, she'd apparently come back to stay for a while. And Cindy and Samantha's sons were becoming friends. His gaze went to the rearview mirror again, and he smiled at the image of the two little boys in the back seat.

"Uncle Brad, you passed the baseball field!"

Brad applied the brakes gingerly and checked his rearview mirror before wheeling the car into a U-turn and heading back to the park.

*   *   *

Samantha returned to the sun room and dropped onto the sofa, still thinking about her encounter with Brad. He was as good-looking as ever, darn it. Maybe better. She'd rather hoped he'd grown fat and bald, but she guessed that was too much to ask. He was only what? Thirty-three? A mental picture of him formed in her mind and a flutter of attraction rippled her midsection. *Stop it, Samantha!* Irritated with herself, she reached for the newspaper. *He's exactly the kind of man you've vowed to avoid.*

Forcing her attention back to the condominium listings, Samantha moved to a nearby desk to make notes on the places that interested her. She would get out to look at them over the upcoming weekend. Then returning to the sofa, she flipped to the front page and tried to concentrate on current news events.

Some time later, the desk clock caught her eye. Five o'clock. She had better start dinner.

In the kitchen, she pulled open the refrigerator door and perused the items she'd purchased at the grocery store that morning: chicken, fish, and salad fixings among them. Deciding on the fish, she closed the door again. She wouldn't have to start that for a while.

The sound of familiar voices drew her to an open window, and she pushed the curtain aside. In the front yard of the Davis home next door, Samantha spied Cindy and her mother, apparently preparing to plant a flower bed. Pots of rust and yellow chrysanthemums stood nearby. They would look lovely against the backdrop of the white, two-story colonial.

Samantha headed outside for a closer look and for a chat with two of her favorite people. Cindy had been her closest friend since childhood, and Mrs. Davis was like a second mother.

Cindy, her husband, and their two children lived in a Detroit suburb now—about an hour from Glen Arbor. She and the kids had spent the past week at her parents' home, however, so that Trevor and Jonathan could become acquainted and Cindy and Samantha could visit.

As Samantha crossed the large expanse of lawn that separated the two houses, the warm sun beat down on her back. But the cool breeze and the puffy clouds that dotted the sky hinted at the approach of autumn.

Engrossed in their task, the two other women didn't notice Samantha's approach until she stood beside them. Then Cindy saw her first. "Hi, Sammy!" She nodded at the flowers. "Aren't they pretty?" She'd begun to describe the design they'd planned for the flower bed when Brad's car pulled into the driveway.

He had no sooner shut off the engine, when his two young passengers exploded out of the back seat. "Mom, you should have seen me hit the ball!" a breathless Jonathan gasped. "Brad showed us how to stand and how to watch the ball come towards us." Samantha opened her mouth to comment, but the two little cyclones dashed off again, this time towards the house and the promise of Grandma's lemonade. Mrs. Davis hurried after them.

Samantha turned to Brad to thank him for his help and found him watching her with an amused expression. "What?" she asked with raised eyebrows.

Humor danced in his eyes. "I see a lot of little Samantha Jane Howard in that bundle of enthusiasm."

The use of her middle name brought back a rush of memories. In their younger years, Brad had used it when he teased her, usually about the freckles he knew she hated. Grinning, she resisted an impulse to touch her nose. "It's Samantha Richards now. I grew up and got married, remember?"

A slow smile spread across his face. "I have to admit I've noticed the growing up part." A hint of flirtation flickered in his eyes, and their gazes held for moment. Then pulling her own away, Samantha retreated to the safety of humor.

"Let me see your hands," she demanded. "Aha, you've grown up too! The last time I saw these, they were covered in grease and pulling weird things from under the hood of that old car you used to drive." She looked up at him in mock wonder. "And to think they've become the hands of a surgeon. Amazing."

Brad laughed. "The old Chevy. Yeah, I was getting it ready to take to college." He frowned, affecting dismay. "That's the most flattering memory you have of me? Covered in grease?"

Cindy approached then, tossing aside a garden trowel. "I think she remembers more than that."

Samantha cringed at the suggestive leer in her friend's voice. Cindy wouldn't!

"Samantha had a giant crush on you back then, you know."

"Cindy!" The gasp of dismay escaped Samantha's lips before she could stop it. Then in an attempt to undo the damage, she tried to mirror Cindy's playfulness. "Don't tell him all of our secrets."

Cindy laughed. "Brad must have known, Samantha. You weren't exactly subtle."

Thankfully, the boys came clamoring into the yard just then, clutching handfuls of Grandma's freshly baked cookies. Jonathan offered one to Brad, which he accepted. In reaching for a second one, proffered by Trevor, Brad caught a glimpse of his watch. "Whoa, it's late! I've got to go." He started towards his car. "Thanks for the cookies, guys." He nodded a good-bye to his sister, and then his gaze seemed to settle softly on Samantha. "See you around, Sam."

"Bye, Brad."

The next moment, he'd swung the SUV out of the driveway and accelerated up the street.

Brad's car had no sooner disappeared around the corner, when a horn sounded from the Howard driveway next door. Samantha turned to see her father climb out of his shiny gray sedan and start towards them, waving something with one hand.

Jonathan ran to him. "Hi, Grampa! What have you got?" Trevor followed and after scrutinizing what Dr. Howard showed them, both boys yelped in enthusiasm. "Mom! Mom! Grampa has tickets to the Detroit Tigers' baseball game. He's going to take Trevor and me on Sunday."

Samantha looked up at her father as he approached. "Cindy and the kids are going back to Bloomfield on Saturday, Dad."

Benton Howard's self-satisfied smile never wavered. "Oh, Cindy won't mind if Trevor stays an extra night. I'll bring him home after the game." His tone implied that the matter was settled.

A doubtful expression furrowed Cindy's brow, but after a brief hesitation, she agreed. Her husband had been looking forward to his family's homecoming, but she guessed he'd understand about the game.

Samantha felt a stir of annoyance at her father's presumptuousness. He should have consulted Cindy before exciting the boys. But as she watched his grin widen at the youngsters' excitement, a pang of guilt replaced her irritation.

He was only enjoying having his grandson here, she told herself. Up to now, he'd spent just a week or two a year with Jonathan on visits to Boston. And when Samantha and her family had visited Michigan, he seemed constantly called away to patient emergencies or to meetings of one kind or another—as he had during Samantha's own childhood. Maybe he was trying to change his priorities. She should be happy about that. Samantha assented to the plan with as much good grace as she could muster.

Late the following morning, Samantha proceeded down the fourth-floor corridor of Michigan University Hospital, scanning the numbers on the office doors. Then she saw it:

Suite 403
Raymond Dwyer, M.D.
Ear, Nose, and Throat

Ear, Nose, and Throat? Her hopes sagged. The friend that told her about this opening for the position of office nurse hadn't mentioned the specialty. Samantha's experience was with a general surgeon. She doubted she'd have much chance of getting this job even if she wanted it. But she couldn't just walk away. She *did* have an appointment. Sighing in resignation, she reached for the doorknob.

Ten minutes later, she sat nodding as Maggie Murphy, the pleasant, gray-haired receptionist and office manager, looked over her resume and explained predictably that they'd hoped to fill the position with someone experienced in the specialty of Ear, Nose, and Throat.

But then Maggie paused and raised an eyebrow. "Although the fact that you've had experience in both a doctor's office and surgery might interest Dr. Dwyer. He's had some problems in the O.R. with inexperienced staff nurses and might appreciate someone who could work with him regularly." She studied the resume again, tapping her pencil on the desktop.

Just then the door opened, and Maggie looked up, flashing a bright smile. "Good morning, doctors! Beautiful day, isn't it?"

Samantha had been sitting with her back to the door and turned now as Maggie proceeded to introduce her. She looked first at a distinguished-looking gentleman of medium height, about sixty years of age, and with graying temples, whom Maggie presented as Dr. Dwyer. He extended his hand and offered a pleasant smile as his office manager informed him that Samantha had come to apply for the position they had open.

Then Maggie introduced Dr. Brad Davis, and Samantha spun around. She and Brad broke into simultaneous grins. "Samantha and I grew up next door to one another," Brad explained to the others.

"Is that right? I'll be darned." Dr. Dwyer reached for Samantha's resume and scanned it.

Samantha felt Brad take a step closer. "If she needs a character reference, Ray, I think I can supply that," his tone reflected tongue-in-cheek humor. "Also her father is our chief of staff."

"Really? I wasn't aware that Benton had a daughter." His eyes crinkled good-naturedly. "I guess we're always too busy talking shop to discuss personal matters."

That sounded like her father all right, Samantha thought.

As Dr. Dwyer continued to peruse the resume, Maggie pointed out an entry to him. "Yes, I noticed that." He turned to Samantha. "Would you be willing to work in surgery with me a few mornings a week, Samantha?"

"Yes, certainly. I'd enjoy it."

He nodded. "We have a few more people to interview, but we'll get back to you as soon as possible." Then moving towards an adjoining hallway, he motioned to Brad. "Come into my office, and I'll show you those x-rays."

Brad's hand came up to press Samantha's arm in encouragement, and he gave her a friendly wink. She tried to ignore the effect of his touch, but her gaze followed him until he had disappeared into Dr. Dwyer's inner office.

Maggie seemed unaware of her distraction and smiled. "We'll call you soon, Samantha."

Thanking her, Samantha left the office.

As she walked slowly towards the elevator, she pondered the details of the job. They appealed to her more than she'd anticipated, despite the fact that she would have to learn this new specialty. Both Dr. Dwyer and Maggie seemed exceptionally pleasant, and the working hours that Maggie described sounded almost too perfect: They were usually finished with office appointments by four o'clock in the afternoon. Dr. Dwyer was anticipating retirement and cutting down on his patient load.

Mulling over these facts, Samantha had stepped into the elevator when she heard someone call her name.

Reaching out to hold open the door, she turned to see Brad hurrying towards her.

He stopped in front of her and placed his hand near hers, against the edge of the impatiently bobbing elevator door. "Do you have time for a cup of coffee? We haven't had much chance to talk since you got back."

"Uh, I'm sorry, Brad, but I left Jonathan with Mrs. Adams, and I hate to take advantage." Best to avoid him as much as possible, considering her attraction to him, she thought. Unfortunately, Brad was exactly the type of man with whom she'd sworn she'd never become involved.

"Mrs. Adams?" He grinned at the mention of their elderly neighbor. "She loves kids. She won't mind a few extra minutes."

Unable to think of another spur-of-the-moment excuse, Samantha assented. "Just a quick cup then. If you're sure *you* have the time."

His dark eyes met hers. "I have the time." Then as if on second thought, he glanced at his watch. "At least I have about thirty minutes."

When the elevator doors had closed them inside, Brad seemed to loom over her in the tiny cubicle. He wore no jacket—only a shirt, tie, and tan slacks—and the obvious breadth of his shoulders, his firm abdomen, and narrow hips gave evidence that he also made time to keep himself in shape. And she could smell his musky aftershave. Samantha found herself enveloped in a cloud of sensual awareness that she hadn't felt in a very long time. She managed with effort to tell him how perfectly the hours at Dr. Dwyer's office would fit her needs. But she remained tense until the door opened, and she could put a little more distance between them.

A few minutes later, they sat at a table in the hospital cafeteria with their cups of steaming coffee between them. "So," Brad began, "apart from the acceptable hours, how does the work you'd do for Ray Dwyer appeal to you?"

"When I first saw the ear, nose, and throat specialty, I thought the job was out of the question. My experience in Boston was with a general surgeon. But I'm having second thoughts. It might be interesting to learn a new area of medicine."

"I'm somewhat familiar with Boston. Where did you work there?"

"Boston General. I was employed by one of the surgeons. Scrubbed with him in the O.R. in the mornings and helped with patients during afternoon office hours. Actually, the situation was similar to the one here: a teaching hospital, associated with a university."

She grimaced. "But I only worked about eight months after finishing school before discovering that I was pregnant with Jonathan. Then I developed complications and had to stop working altogether. I never wanted to go back after he was born." She shrugged. "It's not a lot of experience, but the fact that it involved both office work and surgery seemed to interest Doctor Dwyer. I guess I can hope."

Brad grinned. "For what it's worth, I'll put in a good word for you."

"Thanks." She shifted in her seat as his smile had the predictable effect on her. "Are both Maggie and Doctor Dwyer as nice as they seem?"

"Yeah, they're both good-natured and easygoing. I imagine they'd be very pleasant to work with."

The more Samantha learned about this job, the more interested she became. She wondered why Brad had been in the office. "Is your residency in ENT?"

He shook his head. "General surgery."

"Cindy said you'd already been offered a position with an established group. Do you think you'll take it?"

He shrugged. "We'll see. It's not official yet."

Brad nodded to a doctor who passed their table, then his gaze returned to Samantha. "Are you and Jonathan settling in okay?"

"I guess. As much as we can until we find a place of our own."

"Have you started looking?"

"Just in the paper so far. I plan to check out some of the condominiums over the weekend."

He asked which places she had in mind and told her about a couple of others that she hadn't heard about. They sipped their coffee and then their gazes met.

"You were gone a lot of years," Brad murmured.

"Yes, ten."

"You must have left soon after . . ." He saw the pain in her eyes and stopped.

"After my mother's funeral?" She nodded. "A few months afterward."

"I tried to get back for it, Sam, but that was a bad time for me: the summer before med school. I had a job at one of the hospitals. You know how that goes, they like to know you're dedicated."

A coolness flickered in her eyes. "Oh, yes. I know all about the demands of your profession."

He frowned at the edge in her voice, then decided

he'd imagined it. "Your mother was a kind and gracious woman, Samantha. I was very fond of her."

Moisture filled her eyes. "Yes, she was that. I still miss her very much. I wish Jonathan . . ." Her voice quavered, and she swallowed. ". . . I wish Jonathan had gotten a chance to know her."

A wave of compassion and tenderness washed over him, and without thinking he reached for her hand. "You're like her, Samantha. Gentle yet strong."

She squeezed his fingers, then pulled free. "Thank you. You couldn't have paid me a nicer compliment."

"You've had some rough times the past several years." Losing both a mother and a husband to premature deaths would have proved debilitating to some, but she'd obviously struggled through intact. And now she was trying to raise a young son alone. Admiration and a sense of protectiveness turned his voice husky. "I'm glad you've come home."

"I've gotten pretty good at taking care of myself and Jonathan. But it's good to be back."

He found himself suddenly lost in the soft pools of her gray-blue eyes. Feelings of compassion evolved into less admirable emotions, and he pulled his gaze away. Sitting back in his chair, he cleared his throat.

"Your, uh . . . your father's relieved that you've come home. So that he can give you whatever help you need."

She frowned. "He said that?"

"Well, not in so many words. . . ."

She couldn't restrain a cynical laugh. "I didn't think so." Her gaze turned cool. "My father never worried about me in all the years I was growing up. I doubt he'll start now."

Brad frowned. "You don't really believe that, Samantha." His eyes reflected the gentle reprimand.

She squared her shoulders. "Yes Brad, I do."

"I know he wasn't always able to be there for you, but surely he did the best he could. He's an honorable man."

Samantha's back straightened. How could Brad say that? He knew the circumstances of their home life. For as long as Samantha could remember, she and her mother had run a distant second to her father's medical career. Because of his emotional neglect, Samantha had vowed—while still in her teens—that never would she marry a career-obsessed man. She gazed at Brad with sad irony. *You sing his praises and justify his actions because you're just like him.*

She remembered the day Brad had come over to solicit her father's advice—when he'd first decided on a career in medicine. They'd developed an immediate rapport, which had built steadily over the years. And now, with the culmination of Brad's residency, he would become a contemporary of the eminent Dr. Benton Howard.

Then an earlier scene from the past came to mind: that long-ago afternoon when she had tearfully rushed over to the Davis house in search of Cindy's supportive shoulder to cry upon. Her father had just canceled their summer plans to leave the very next day to spend a week—which included her twelfth birthday—at a house on Lake Michigan. It was to have been their first family vacation in years. She remembered her chagrin at finding Brad at home alone. But, to her surprise, he'd consoled her patiently. She still vividly remembered that teenage boy's quiet understanding and soothing words of consolation to an awkward and heartbroken adolescent.

Was that when it began? Her adulation of the boy next door? How could he have changed so?

Just then, a clock on the wall caught her eye. "Uh-oh. Looks like your half-hour's up. And I'd better run too. I don't want to take advantage of Mrs. Adams."

They drained their cups and exited the cafeteria. Outside, Brad ran a hand through his hair in a gesture of uncharacteristic nervousness. "Uh, Samantha, I was wondering if you'd have dinner with me one night this week. Thursday or Friday, maybe? I have to work the weekend."

She paused, taken by surprise. "I, uh . . . I'm sorry, Brad, but this is a hectic week." She had no intention of dating this man.

"You're busy both nights?"

Samantha looked him in the eye. "My father doesn't spend much time at home, and I hate to leave Jonathan with sitters too often. Especially so soon after our move."

"Can I stop over for a while then?"

"Really, it's a bad week." She saw the disappointment in his eyes and steeled herself against weakening. Best to let him know where she stood right away.

"Can I give you a call after you've had a chance to get settled then?"

"Uh . . . I suppose, if you like." However, she purposefully injected a note of disinterest in her tone.

Brad's beeper went off just then, and he hurried off to catch a closing elevator.

Chapter Two

On Sunday morning, the day of the much-anticipated baseball game, Samantha and Jonathan had just finished their cereal when a knock sounded at the back door. Samantha answered it, then stepped aside as Trevor burst into the kitchen, clutching a Detroit Tigers' T-shirt. "Want to wear my Tigers shirt, Jon? Then we'll both look cool at the game!" Trevor himself sported a baseball hat with the same logo.

Jonathan jumped down from his chair. "Yeah! Neat-o!" The two youngsters scurried towards Jonathan's bedroom with Jon struggling to remove the shirt he'd donned earlier. A few minutes later they returned, announcing that they would wait out in the backyard until Grandpa was ready to leave for the ball game.

As Samantha cleared the breakfast dishes, the dull cracks of Jonathan's whiffle ball, hitting his plastic bat, drifted in through the open window. A cheer of enthusiasm or groan of woe followed each crack. She smiled at the exuberance of the two little boys.

And she smiled in tolerant amusement every fifteen minutes thereafter as they ran into the house to ask how much longer before Grandpa was ready to go.

Samantha's father spent most of the morning in his study, apparently much of the time on the telephone, since she'd heard it ring several times. Then about an hour before he and the boys were scheduled to leave for the ball game, Dr. Howard emerged with a serious, no-nonsense expression on his face. Samantha knew that look all too well and braced herself for what she suspected would follow.

"Samantha, I'm afraid I won't be able to take the boys to the ball game today after all."

"Oh, Dad . . ." She heard the frustration and reprimand in her voice and paused, knowing a reaction of that sort would surely lead to conflict.

And indeed, he appeared annoyed. A tall, handsome, and imposing man, he carried himself with an air of indisputable authority. This demeanor and the respect he'd earned within his profession ensured that he rarely encountered anything but compliance with his wishes. Directing a scowl of displeasure at his daughter, he spoke curtly.

"Just explain to Jonathan and Trevor that I had some important business come up. They'll understand." Then tucking a folder underneath an arm that already carried his briefcase, he headed for the front door.

She followed, concern for two little boys propelling her forward. "They won't understand, Dad!" He whirled to face her, irritation flashing in his eyes, and

Samantha took an unintentional step backward before planting her feet. "They've been so excited about the game, and Trevor stayed an extra night in order to go. Isn't there anything you can do?"

"Surely after all these years, you realize the importance of my work." He reached into his pocket and pulled out the tickets, handing them to her. "Here, *you* take the boys to the ball game. As long as they get to go, why should it matter who takes them?"

Samantha strove to control her resentment. She had become used to this kind of disappointment while growing up, but in view of the traumatic turmoil of the past two years, she'd have expected even her father to be more considerate of her son. "Jonathan was excited about going with *you*, Dad. A small child needs some measure of predictability in his life."

Her father's thoughtlessness had also complicated her own plans. "Besides, I have another job interview tomorrow, and I'd planned to polish my resume today." She resisted the inclination to wither under his stern gaze. "I also wanted to start looking at condominiums this afternoon. I purposely kept the day free to do these things."

"For heaven's sake, Samantha, those are trivialities!" The words erupted from him, and he pulled himself to his full height. "There is absolutely no hurry. You know that you and Jonathan can live here as long as you like. And you certainly don't need to begin working right away."

"I intend to be independent, Dad. And I want to live in a neighborhood with children close to Jonathan's age." *And I especially don't want him growing up in an atmosphere like this, where everyone else's activ-*

*ities and interests are denigrated when compared
against the eminent Dr. Howard's.*

"We'll talk about this later. I don't have time to
argue now." He turned and left the house.

Samantha stared at the slammed door in helpless
frustration. A moment later, she heard his car start,
and familiar tears of resentment filled her eyes. She
thought of all the years that she and her mother'd had
to endure this kind of thoughtless disregard from him.

Except that her mother had always accepted his actions with an infinite degree of love and understanding. Elizabeth Howard had sacrificed much of what
she, herself, wanted in her relatively short life to the
demands of his practice and to the various additional
responsibilities he undertook to enhance his position
in the medical community: prestigious staff positions,
speaking engagements, medical society leadership
roles, authorship of books and articles, and for a short
time, even a series of guest spots on a radio talk show.

Images flashed through Samantha's mind: of her
mother, wrapped in a robe and curled up with a book
on the living room sofa, waiting until all hours for him
to come home; her mother's soothing smile and gentle
consolation as she explained to Samantha the cancellation of yet another family outing.

Familiar waves of sadness and grief washed over
her. Her mother's early death—having realized so few
of her own desires—had been the final catalyst. Soon
afterward, Samantha had left her father's house,
choosing to attend a college on the east coast.

Had she been a fool to return now?

No. This town was her home, and she wouldn't let
him keep her away. She would, however, accept the
fact that he'd never change. She would find herself

and Jonathan a place of their own, get her son away from his grandfather's influence as soon as possible.

With a firm nod at the finality of her decision, Samantha went outside to find the boys and explain the change in plans.

A week later, Brad pulled off his sterile gown, hurled it into a hamper, and exited the operating room in a fit of pique. He'd finished this surgical procedure only thirty seconds ago, and already she'd invaded his thoughts.

He hadn't seen Samantha since that day in the cafeteria over a week ago. He'd sensed her cool reaction to his dinner invitation and had resisted calling her. But he didn't know how long he could continue to do so. Attractiveness aside, something about her pulled at him.

He walked to a window off the hallway and stood, looking outside, trying to calm his emotions. Then his gaze settled on a head of long, blond hair in the parking lot. *Oh great. Now he was seeing her too.*

But wait. That was her! Talking to another woman. Could he get down there in time?

He tore for the stairway. He sure as heck could try.

His feet flew down the stairs, jumping the last three or four at each landing. Geez, six flights. Keep talking, Samantha.

Arriving at the first floor, he raced down the corridor, passing curious onlookers. When he burst out into the parking lot, he came to halt and squinted in the bright sunlight. There she stood, dead ahead, not twenty feet away and still talking.

He pulled deep breaths into his panting lungs and continued towards her, feigning casualness.

"Well hi, Samantha. How's the job hunt going?"

She wrinkled her nose. "Not very well. I've just come from two more interviews, and both offices require longer hours than I can even consider. I ran into the same problem yesterday."

"What about Dwyer's office? Haven't you heard from them?"

She shook her head. "Not a word."

"Why don't you call them? Bug' em a little."

"I intend to. Especially now that I know what a rare opportunity that job is." She paused. "I do have one more appointment out at the office complex on Washington, but that would be a half-hour commute each way."

Washington? Cripes, he'd never see her if she worked way out there. He'd better have a talk with his old pal, Dwyer.

"I'm sorry," Samantha's gaze moved between her companion and Brad. "Have you two met?"

"I know who Dr. Davis is, of course," the other woman purred, "but he probably doesn't remember me. I work at the front desk in admitting." When Brad turned to the woman, he found her gazing up at him with an expression of . . . uh-oh! Brad took a reflexive step backward as she extended a carefully groomed hand.

Forcing himself to take it, Brad cast a wary glance at Samantha and got an unexpected surprise: that look in her eye—was it jealousy? *Maybe he'd just take advantage of this situation.*

He intentionally injected a warmth into his smile as he turned back to the woman. "Sure I remember you. I get down your way often." He allowed the woman to hold his gaze for several seconds longer than necessary.

"I'll just let you two get acquainted." Samantha's voice interrupted his performance. "I have a million things to do." She turned on her heel.

"Uh, Samantha!" Brad tried to pull his hand loose, encountered resistance, and yanked it free. But Samantha's car was just a few feet away, and she'd already climbed inside. Starting the motor, she gave a brief wave and drove off.

Brad slapped the fender of a nearby car in frustration as he watched her disappear around a bend. Then turning back towards the hospital, he encountered the heated gaze of Ms. Admitting. Making a wide circle around her, he started towards the building. "I . . . have to rush off, myself. Got to see a guy about . . . something."

Samantha didn't have to call Dr. Dwyer's office. Maggie called her the next day. "We'd like you to join our staff if you're still interested."

She started the following Monday and rapidly became familiar with the routine. Samantha and the doctor spent three mornings a week in surgery and the remaining mornings and every afternoon in the office, seeing patients.

And Samantha enjoyed learning the new specialty. Dr. Dwyer performed much of his ear surgery under a microscope and frequently stepped aside to invite Samantha to view the surgical field and the various steps of each procedure. She found the intricate work fascinating. And, as she'd expected, both Dr. Dwyer and Maggie proved to be pleasant co-workers.

On the Friday afternoon of her first week on the

job, Samantha stood near the front desk, jotting some notes on a patient's chart when the telephone rang.

Maggie took the call and after a few words of greeting, looked over at Samantha and winked before continuing. "I'm sorry, but the position's been filled. Dr. Dwyer wanted someone with surgical as well as office experience, and we had two applicants with both."

When Maggie had completed the call, Samantha cast her a look of interest and surprise. "There were two of us with surgical experience?"

"Yes. Actually, the other applicant looked awfully good," Maggie teased. "But then Brad came in pleading your case, and well," she shrugged, "Dr. Dwyer is a good friend of his parents. What could he say?"

Samantha's mouth dropped open in dismay.

Maggie laughed. "I'm kidding, Samantha. Your qualifications and references were too good to pass up." She gave her a look of admiration. "First in your nursing school graduating class! Very impressive. With such obvious ability and dedication, I'm surprised your father didn't talk you into medical school."

Samantha hoisted a pile of charts into her arms. "That's another story. I'll tell you about it some time." She started towards the filing cabinet, then paused and frowned. "Brad came here to plead my case?"

Maggie feigned intense seriousness. "Oh my, yes. Actually you've got quite a reputation to uphold. According to Brad, in addition to having a fervent interest in this job, you're also intelligent, congenial, industrious, and loyal." She suppressed a tongue-in-cheek smile. "Quite a perfect person in every way. I kept expecting him to add 'attractive' to his list, but I guess he thought it unnecessary to mention that obvious fact."

Samantha felt herself color. "I . . . I'll have to be sure and thank Doctor Davis."

Maggie's smile burst free of restraint, and she chuckled. "So will I, Samantha. So will I."

That evening, Samantha pulled the bed covers over her son's shoulders and listened with interest as he described the activities of his five-day stay at Trevor's house. Cindy had invited Jonathan to spend this last week before the start of school with them so that Samantha could begin her new job without worrying about his welfare.

Cindy's husband, Bob, had brought Jonathan home just a few hours before, and Jonathan had been talking nonstop ever since. As he snuggled under the covers now, exhausted by a busy week of play and several hours of chatter, Samantha kissed him on the forehead, then bade him good-night and tiptoed from the room.

This last week had been a busy one for her too. After much looking, she'd found a condominium complex nearby. Actually, it was one that Brad had suggested, and its only drawback was that their one foreseeable vacancy would not become available for six weeks. Samantha had decided that the advantages of the place outweighed the inconvenience of waiting, however, and agreed to take it. Her father had assured her that he welcomed her company and Jonathan's for the additional time; however, he was around so seldom that it sometimes seemed that she and her son lived alone in the big house.

Entering her own bedroom now, Samantha pulled a box of old nursing textbooks from the back of her closet, searching specifically for her anatomy and physiology books and anything else that would give her more insight into the specialty of Ear, Nose, and Throat. She was finding her work with Dr. Dwyer fascinating, and now that she knew both he and Maggie had high expectations of her, she wanted to make a supreme effort. In appreciation of their confidence.

Which reminded her there was someone else to whom she owed a few words of appreciation. She walked to the telephone and stood looking down at it. This would be a lot easier if she hadn't treated Brad so brusquely the last few times she'd seen him.

With a sigh of resignation, she wiped her dusty hands on her jeans and picked up the phone, first calling information and then dialing Brad's number.

He didn't answer until the fourth ring, and then his hoarse voice came on the line. "Yeah. Dr. Davis."

"Brad? Uh-oh! I'm sorry, did I wake you?" She glanced at the clock. It was only nine-fifteen.

He sounded groggy. "I don't know. Yeah, I guess so."

"I'm sorry. It's Samantha."

She heard a rustle at the other end of the line, and when he spoke again, he sounded more alert. "What can I do for you, Sam?"

"I just wanted to thank you, but I can call back."

"No, it's all right. I'm on duty again in an hour anyway." He paused. "Thank me for what?"

"For suggesting the Glenview condominiums. We're going to take one."

"Oh yeah? Good. I'm glad that worked out."

"And for putting in a good word for me with Dr. Dwyer. I got the job."

"Hey, that's great! But I think they'd already decided. Besides, all I did is tell them what I know about you."

She laughed. "All of my virtues and none of my faults, apparently."

A moment of silence followed, then he spoke in a low, husky voice. "If you have any faults, I'm not aware of them."

A flood of warmth at his tone of intimacy disconcerted her. After another moment of silence, she grasped for something to say. "I've enjoyed the job so far. It's all so new and interesting. But I've got a lot to learn. I was just going through some of my old textbooks for information on ENT."

"Have you been able to find enough? I'm sure I have something from my rotation in the service. I could drop it by if it'd help."

Touched by his thoughtfulness, she couldn't bear to rebuff him again. Besides, she could use the information. "That would be great, Brad, but I hate to put you out. Could you leave it at the hospital for me somewhere?"

"It's no problem. I need to run by my parents' house this weekend anyway. I'll bring whatever I can find then."

"Thanks, I'd appreciate that."

Another brief pause.

"You liked the Glenview complex, huh?"

"Yes, very much. The grounds are so neat and attractive, and you were right about the family atmosphere. Jonathan's excited about all the kids we saw playing there. There's just one drawback." She told him about the delay in moving in. "But we think it's worth the wait. The moving van arrives from the east coast tomorrow, but they've agreed to drop off the few essentials we need immediately and then store the rest until our new place is ready."

She remembered that he had to be at the hospital soon. "I'm keeping you, Brad. You probably have to get ready to go."

"I'm all right. I've got a little time. What will you do about starting Jonathan in school if you can't move into your new place for awhile?"

His interest sounded genuine, and she couldn't resist the urge to share her experiences with someone who cared. She hadn't had a good friend to talk to since Cindy left.

"That part's kind of exciting. The condominiums are in the same school district as the house here, so he'll go to the school that *we* all went to." Her words began to tumble out. "Did you know that sweet Mrs. Randolph still teaches first grade? He'll have her too!" They talked about teachers who had taught various other grades and found that they'd had several in common. When they'd progressed to discussing junior high and then high school, Samantha again remembered the time.

"Oh, Brad, I'd really better let you go now." She laughed. "I'm sorry, I got carried away. It's been fun talking." She apologized again for waking him and thanked him once more for his help in influencing Dr. Dwyer. "And I'll look forward to getting whatever ENT information you have."

After she'd hung up, the silence of the house seemed to close around her again. She'd enjoyed their chat, and the quiet that engulfed her now left her feeling lonely by comparison.

Then as her thoughts drifted back over their conversation, the memory of his low, intimate murmur stirred a sensation of longing, which she determinedly pushed from her mind. But she couldn't extinguish the craving for companionship and conversation. They'd get another chance to talk when he brought the books. Was it possible they could just be good friends?

Late the following Sunday afternoon, Brad turned off the ignition of his car in the curved driveway of the Howards' Tudor-style home and sat looking at it through a haze of fatigue. He'd always liked the old place. The buff-colored brick, combined with gray-blue roof tiles and shutters, gave it a look of solid elegance.

He ran a weary hand over his face and sighed. If he sat here admiring it much longer, he'd fall asleep. His eyes felt as though someone had thrown sand into them.

Brad had hoped to spend a little time with Samantha today, but he'd unexpectedly had to stay on duty for the better part of an additional shift. Now fatigue was like a massive weight he hauled around, and he had to get some sleep. He'd just drop off the books and leave.

Ever since her phone call on Friday night, he'd had more difficulty than ever getting Samantha out of his mind. Their conversation seemed to open a corridor of intimacy between them, and he'd had to force himself to wait this long before contacting her again. When he was with patients, thoughts of her hovered on the periphery of his awareness, rushing back when his mind became free. He couldn't ever remember a woman affecting him this way before. No one else ever made concentrating on work an effort.

But spending time with her would have to wait. He'd just gone almost thirty-six hours without sleep and had to be back on duty at midnight. Glancing at his watch, he groaned: four o'clock already. Brad rubbed his gritty eyes, grabbed the books from the seat, and pushed himself up and out of the car. Plodding heavily to the door, he rang the bell and leaned against the doorjamp.

When the door opened, Samantha's gray-blue eyes smiled up at him. She wore denim shorts and a white T-shirt, and the look on her face was one of undisguised pleasure. "Hi, Brad!" Her gaze dropped to the bundle he carried. "Are those the books?"

A spurt of adrenaline shot him upright, and he mumbled an affirmative answer as she took them from him.

"Thank you for bringing them over." She stepped aside. "Can you come in?"

"Just for a minute." She looked so freshly scrubbed that he felt self-conscious about the stubble that he knew darkened his face. He hadn't seen her in almost two weeks, and he swore she'd gotten more beautiful in the meantime.

"Hi Brad!" An exuberant Jonathan bounded toward him. "Our stuff came from Boston yesterday." Two large cardboard boxes stood against the wall of the foyer. "Wanna come to my room and see my toys?"

Brad forced himself to sound interested. "Sure. Let's take a look." He saw Samantha's smile of apology as he followed Jonathan numbly towards his bedroom.

The boy shoved one toy after another into Brad's hands and proceeded to give him a short history of each. As he sat on the bed, examining the model F-16 fighter plane, the features of which Jonathan knowledgeably explained, Brad realized that Samantha had followed them into the room. She gave him a concerned frown.

"You look dead on your feet, Brad. When was the last time you got a good night's sleep?"

Even his answering laugh took a conscious effort. "I can't remember." He pushed himself to his feet.

"Jonathan, honey, you can show Brad the rest of your toys another time. He's very tired now."

"Okay. But hey, Brad, just let me show you one more thing—my new wooden bat and softball." He retrieved them from the closet and held them up, looking with longing into Brad's face. "Maybe sometime we could go to the park again. When Trevor comes. Or maybe even if he doesn't come."

Brad grinned. "Sure. We'll do that." He took the bat from Jonathan. "Let's see what kind you've got there." He turned it around in his hands. "Pretty neat, Jon."

Samantha watched her son's eyes dance. In view of Brad's obvious exhaustion, his patience amazed Samantha.

He picked up the softball too, then tossed it back to the youngster. "We'll try them out soon."

Shoving both back into the closet, Jonathan ran to his desk drawer and pulled out a pad and pencil. "I'll go copy our phone number so you can call me when you have time to play." He scurried out of the room.

Brad watched him go with an amused smile. "That's a nice kid you've got there."

"I agree. Think I'll keep him."

As they followed Jonathan towards the kitchen, Brad glanced through the open doorway of another bedroom. It contained a canopied bed with a white eyelet comforter. Chinese design area rugs covered the hardwood floor in several places. The few bottles of perfume on the mirrored dresser confirmed his suspicion that this was Samantha's bedroom. He wondered which of those fragrances she wore now that wafted provocatively to his nostrils and caused his tired blood to stir.

When they arrived back in the foyer, he pushed at the moving boxes with the toe of his shoe. "Do you have room to unpack all of this stuff here?"

"Grandpa doesn't like them in the house," Jonathan told him. "We tried to push these two big ones out to the garage, but they're too heavy."

"What? These?" Brad walked over to them and tested their weight. "I can take these out for you."

Samantha protested, citing his fatigue, but he lifted the first one easily. "Where do you want them?"

She showed him to a corner of the garage, where he deposited the box and then went back for the second one. Returning to the kitchen, he looked around. "Anything else I can help you with?"

"No thanks. We can manage now." She watched him with concern, and he remembered that the last time he'd looked in a mirror, the dark circles around his eyes had reminded him of a raccoon. He rubbed them self-consciously.

"There's more boxes in the sun room."

Samantha turned to her son in mild exasperation. "Those are fine right where they are, Jonathan."

Brad started for the sun room. "I'll get them."

"No, Brad, you're exhausted."

"It's no trouble."

"Brad, please don't." She rushed forward and reached that corner of the room just in time to inject herself between him and the boxes. "Really, they're fine," she spread her hands against his chest and tried to push him back.

But he couldn't move. They stood so close that he caught another whiff of her delicate scent. And he could feel her warmth. When she looked up at him, he saw awareness in her eyes too, and for a long moment, their gazes locked and held.

Then sliding from the confined space, she gripped one of his arms in both her hands and pulled him away. "I was just going to fix Jonathan and myself a snack. Will you have something with us? I can have it ready in a few minutes." She sounded matter-of-fact, but he could see the flush in her cheeks.

He wasn't hungry, but he welcomed the excuse to stay for a few more minutes. Thanking her, he sank down onto the nearby sofa.

Before proceeding to the kitchen, Samantha cast another concerned glance in his direction. "When do you have to be back at the hospital?"

"Midnight," he told her and saw her grimace.

She left the room, and Brad slumped down into the softness of the cushions. If he wasn't careful, he could fall asleep here in a minute. Jonathan climbed up beside him, and as the boy described his excitement at the prospect of starting school the next day, Brad closed his eyes for just a second. And the sound of Jonathan's voice faded slowly away.

Then, through an exhausted haze, Brad became aware of someone jostling his legs. He tried to rouse himself, but failed and slipped again into oblivion.

The next sound he heard was the rustle of paper. He forced his eyes open to the blurry image of a newspaper, opened across the width of a nearby chair. His gaze dropped to the long, shapely legs that stretched from the bottom of the paper to the floor, and a stir of attraction moved through him.

Brad shifted, and Samantha peered over the top of the newspaper. "Go back to sleep." Her tone feigned authority.

"What time is it?" A low light glowed next to her chair, and he saw that darkness had fallen outside.

"Ten o'clock."

He let his head fall back onto the sofa pillow. "Oh man!" He tried to rouse himself. "I've got to get up."

Samantha threw the paper aside and hurried towards him. "Don't, Brad. You're obviously exhausted."

When he pushed himself to a half-sitting position, she perched on the edge of the couch beside him and attempted to force his shoulders down. "I'll wake you at eleven. Go back to sleep."

Resisting the pressure with little effort, he smiled at her. "Bossy little thing, aren't you?"

"Yes! Sleep!"

He let himself fall back against the pillow under the weight of her hands as a cloud of blond hair fell across one of her cheeks. They smiled at each other playfully, and he reached up to push the hair out of her face. "Sleep?" he murmured. "With you sitting here next to me? Not a chance."

Her hand stirred on his shoulder, but she didn't pull away. Their eyes met and held. Slowly he pushed his fingers into her hair. His thumb moved gently over the softness of her cheek. He saw a yearning in her eyes, and then for a moment, it seemed to battle with wariness. Raising his free hand to her shoulder, he urged her downward.

When their lips touched, heat raced through him. He slid his hand to the back of her neck and pulled her mouth more firmly against his own. She returned his kiss.

Then suddenly, almost frantically, she wrenched her mouth free. Sitting upright, she gazed at him with a shaken expression, then stood and backed away. "I'm sorry. I shouldn't have . . ."

He struggled to his feet. "It's okay, Sam. I'm sorry too."

"I never meant for that to happen, Brad."

"I understand." Obviously it was too soon. The memories of her husband must still be strong. But he could wait. His churning emotions told him he'd wait forever if necessary.

"Maybe you should leave."

"If that's what you want." But his feet wouldn't move. "Can I call you?"

"I don't think so, Brad. I'm not ready for this. And even when I am . . ." She gazed up at him with an apologetic expression.

A sick feeling twisted in his gut. "Are you trying to tell me I'm not your type?"

"I don't think you are. I'm sorry."

"Come on, Samantha. I didn't imagine it. We both felt something when I kissed you."

She took a step backwards. "I can't start this kind of relationship with you, Brad. Now or ever."

"Why not?"

"Because you're exactly the kind of man I've promised myself to avoid."

"What kind is that?"

"Someone whose first priority will always be his job. His career."

"I haven't developed a set of priorities, yet. Haven't even had time to think about it."

"I think you set them the day you decided to become a doctor."

He expelled a long breath. Looked down at the floor for a moment and then back up at her. "Shades of your father? Is that what you're thinking?"

"Maybe."

"Look Samantha, wait until you know me better and then judge me as an individual, okay?"

He saw the curtain of detachment descend in her eyes. "I'm sorry, Brad. I won't change my mind."

"I'd like a chance to at least try and change it."

She shook her head. "Really, there's no point."

He met her gaze and held it. "Honey, I'll try anyway. I won't be able to help myself." He walked to the door and opened it, then looked back at her. "Good-bye, Samantha. For now."

The following week went smoothly, thanks to the efforts of several people who cooperated with Samantha in synchronizing her own and Jonathan's routine. His teacher arranged for him to stay at school an extra hour, and since the house was only two blocks away, he was then able to walk home by himself. And Maggie offered to cover for Samantha on those rare occasions when office hours extended a few minutes longer than usual so that she could count on being home on time. They would schedule the more difficult cases for early afternoon, leaving routine appointments for later, which Maggie could easily handle alone if necessary. As a result, Samantha and Jonathan arrived home at the same time each day.

On Saturday morning, with her father away again, and Jonathan occupied with cartoons, Samantha luxuriated in a warm shower and washed her hair. As she came out of the bathroom, clad in a terry-cloth robe and towel turban, Jonathan accosted her, leaping gleefully.

"Mom! Brad called while you were in the shower, and we're going to the park to hit balls this afternoon." He paused. "If it's all right with you, Brad said." Then boundless enthusiasm leaped back into the gray-blue eyes, so like Samantha's own. "I can go, can't I, Mom?"

How could she say no?

"Brad said he'd come about three o'clock."

Overcome with excitement, Jonathan ate very little lunch. Afterward, he gathered his supplies: bat, ball, glove, baseball hat, and sweatshirt, checking and rechecking them repeatedly during the course of the afternoon. And he watched the clock, going to the window every few minutes to look for Brad as three o'clock approached.

But he still waited and watched at three-thirty. And four o'clock.

Then the telephone rang. A nurse from surgery had a message for Jonathan. Brad was involved in a difficult case, but he'd call Jon as soon as he finished. Maybe they could still get to the park for a while before dinner.

But five o'clock came and then five-thirty, and still Brad didn't call. Finally, a little after six, the telephone rang. Jonathan rushed to answer it, and Samantha picked up the extension.

It was Brad this time, and he explained that they'd just finished the surgical case that had delayed him. He still couldn't leave, however. Another emergency had come in, and he was the only one around qualified to handle it. It would detain him until after dark. He apologized to Jonathan but promised to take him to the park the following day, instead. "Ask your Mom if tomorrow afternoon's all right."

"I'm on the line, Brad." Samantha's first inclination was to tell him to forget the whole thing, but Jonathan's eager voice preempted her.

"Tomorrow's okay, huh Mom?" He sounded so hopeful that she swallowed her refusal and agreed half-heartedly. Then Brad had to rush back to work.

But the next afternoon, a similar scenario repeated itself, and Samantha watched with barely controlled fury as Jonathan once again put his bat, ball, glove, and clothes back into his closet, his small shoulders drooping with disappointment. Why had she agreed to this charade? When would she ever learn?

She hid her anger for Jonathan's sake, however, and in order to take his mind off his disappointment, made a big production of fixing cups of hot chocolate before bedtime. He cooperated, but without enthusiasm.

Brad called back at ten o'clock, after Jonathan had gone to bed, to apologize to Samantha. As she listened to the well-worn excuses, a familiar sense of helpless frustration settled over her.

No more, she told herself. She wouldn't stand by while her son suffered the same disappointments and rejections that she'd experienced while growing up. She would put an end to it now.

But first, she had an overwhelming desire to impress upon Brad the disappointment he'd caused. In detail, she described how excitedly Jonathan had anticipated the outings on both days, how he had watched the clock as the hours of waiting passed, and how disappointed he had been when Brad finally canceled. The retelling of it firmed her protective instincts.

"I realize that these inconveniences are part of a doctor's life, Brad. My father has already canceled a trip to a ball game with Jonathan since our return. I wonder if either of you realize how disappointing these last-minute cancellations are for a small child?" Brad started to speak, but she refused to allow him to interrupt. "I think it's best if you didn't make any more plans with Jonathan. Especially now, before he's made friends here. He looks forward to these outings too intensely."

"Look, Samantha, I'm sorry. Both days, I honestly thought I'd be able to get away without any trouble." She heard him sigh in frustration. "The circumstances were unavoidable."

"I'm sure that's true, Brad, and that's just the point. They're unavoidable for you. But I can avoid them. For Jonathan and myself. And I intend to."

"Samantha . . ."

"I've made up my mind, Brad. Please don't make any more plans with my son."

An extended pause followed, and he expelled another long breath. "Alright, I'll do as you ask. But I promised him that I'd phone again soon. Will you explain for me?"

"I'll take care of it. I'll tell him that you're very busy right now. Thank you for understanding."

"Can I call in a few weeks? To see how you're both doing?"

She thought of his help in securing the job with Dr. Dwyer and his kindness to Jonathan in the past. Also she sincerely believed that his intentions for these outings had been honorable, even if his judgment was flawed.

"Alright, yes. In a few weeks."
They ended the conversation on a courteous note.

Samantha passed Brad in the hospital corridors over
the next several days, and they spoke politely but always briefly. On one occasion, he appeared about to
say more, but a colleague approached him, and Samantha moved on.

On Thursday morning, Samantha and Dr. Dwyer
finished their surgical cases early. One of their patients
had developed a cold, necessitating the delay of a
planned procedure. After pulling the sterile drape from
the operating room microscope and gathering the con-
taminated instruments for re-sterilization, Samantha
sauntered to the head nurse's office to check out their
surgical schedule for the following day.

Entering the empty office, she glanced at the clock.
It was only eleven, and afternoon office hours didn't
start until two. She began to ponder what to do with
the unexpected free time.

Suddenly the head nurse came rushing into the
room. She appeared frantic, checking over the list of
ongoing surgical cases and comparing them with her
list of available personnel.

"Darn it! I don't have anyone to send in there!"

"Problem?" Samantha asked.

"Doctor Davis is starting an emergency bleeding ulcer in room two without a scrub nurse. The patient's
hemorrhaging badly, and they have to go right in.
They need some help, and I have no one to send
them." She picked up the phone and then slammed it
down again. "There's no time to call anybody from
home. What am I going to do?"

"I'll go," Samantha offered.

When the flustered nurse turned an inquisitive gaze to her, Samantha explained. "I had eight months of experience in general surgery over at Boston General. I know the instruments."

Relief flooded the distressed woman's features. "Oh, Samantha, that's great! Go scrub! I'll tell them you're coming."

Tucking a stray tendril of hair into her surgical cap, Samantha re-secured her mask over her nose and mouth and rushed to the scrub room. The minutes of required scrub time seemed an eternity, knowing what was likely happening in that operating room. As the hands on the clock edged towards the final seconds, Samantha rinsed her hands and snapped the water off at the control near her knee. Hands above her elbows, she backed through the door into the operating room.

Chapter Three

Pandemonium reigned within. Brad and another physician stood on either side of the operating table, working feverishly over the draped and anesthetized patient. Blood flooded the surgical field. Brad's assistant virtually bailed the crimson liquid from the site of the incision. An anesthesiologist at the patient's head frowned at his set of instruments, repeatedly taking the man's blood pressure. Bloodied surgical knives, hemostats, and other instruments littered the patient's abdomen close to the open wound.

Samantha slipped hurriedly into a sterile gown, which the head nurse tied behind her, then pulled on sterile gloves. Approaching Brad's side of the table, she began clearing the surgical site of the soiled instruments, returning them to the table and tray from which she would work.

"Suction! Sponges!" Brad's voice cracked with tension. The assisting resident inserted an elongated suction tip into the incision, and Samantha ripped open pack after pack of gauze four-by-fours, spilling them to the side of the open wound, within Brad's easy reach.

"Pack them in there, Greg," Brad directed the junior resident. "If we can staunch this flow for just a few seconds, maybe I can see where the blasted thing is."

"Snap," he requested, holding open his hand. And Samantha slapped one hemostat after another into his open palm, watching as he applied them to pinch off bleeding blood vessels. He worked coolly and skillfully.

"Are you giving him blood?" Brad flicked a quick glance at the anesthesiologist. "He's losing a lot of it here."

"Sure am. Pressure's still dropping though."

"We can't lose this guy. He's got a wife and four kids." As another blurb of blood surged upward, Brad's voice took on a more intense note of urgency. "I can't find the thing! We need to widen the field." He shot a desperate glance at the instrument table.

Samantha's hand moved quickly. "Kelley retractor?" She handed him the large instrument.

"Good, let's try that." He inserted it into the wound and asked her to hold it in place. She had to lean over and reach under one of his arms to do so.

"Much better. Can you keep the hemostats coming?" She managed to do so with her free hand.

"There it is!" He could see the ulcer now. "Let's get these last few bleeders pinched off, and we'll take care of this baby." They worked swiftly and silently, and as they gained control of the situation, their tension eased. "Hang in there, Mike," Brad addressed the unconscious patient. "We're getting you fixed up here."

Samantha watched Brad's skilled hands move in fluid rhythm. Her gaze moved to his face, and she saw the intense concentration.

This is what he'd been doing last Saturday and Sunday when he'd disappointed Jonathan. When she'd accused him of carelessly disregarding her son's feelings. He'd been saving lives.

A pang of guilt seized her. As a nurse, she should have stopped to think about that. Should have shown more understanding and encouraged Jonathan to do the same.

Or should she?

Brad's obvious skill and admirable dedication didn't change the fact that his personal time would never be his own. The people that shared his life would have to be continuously understanding of that fact. She supposed some could do that, but unfortunately, she wasn't one of them. Nor did she care to be. Or want her son to be.

Maybe that made her selfish and unfeeling, but she couldn't help it. Her attitude had evolved from years of dispiriting experiences, and she couldn't change. She wouldn't want to if she could.

As the repair work drew to an end, Brad's adrenaline level subsided, and the pace of his movements slowed, though he continued to work steadily. He couldn't help a deep feeling of satisfaction at the fact that he'd been able to pull this husband and father through his crisis. He whispered a prayer of thanks for his ability to do so.

God, he loved this work.

He'd enjoyed the science of medicine in medical school, but since the day he first walked into an operating room, his interest in surgery had surpassed everything else in life. He lived it, breathed it. Thought about very little else.

At least he had until recently. The past few weeks, a new distraction had been vying for his attention.

"Fine job, Brad." The anesthesiologist interrupted his thoughts.

Brad acknowledged the compliment with a nod as he surveyed his work one last time. The only thing left to do was close the wound.

As he straightened and flexed the tension from his shoulders, Brad became aware of a familiar scent. Something about it sharpened his senses. He shook his head and tried to put it out of his mind. "Okay, let's close. We'll use . . ." he turned to the nurse and found a needle, already clamped in a holder, being handed to him. He looked up in surprise and found himself looking into familiar gray-blue eyes.

"3–0 gut?" she asked.

"Uh, yeah, that's great." For a moment, he could only stare.

The anesthesiologist's voice brought him back again. "Blood pressure's back up and steady now."

They began the process of closing, working almost mechanically. But Brad was now intensely aware of the woman beside him. Her movements were swift and efficient—and profoundly disturbing as she occasionally brushed against him. He straightened and backed away from the table, addressing the younger resident. "Go ahead, Greg. Finish closing."

He stood watching for a moment, then stepped away and removed his sterile gown and gloves. He went to stand at the head of the operating table to check the patient's vital signs with the anesthesiologist. Old Mike was stabilizing nicely.

When the resident had completed the closing, Brad watched him wheel the patient out of the room. Then his gaze sought out the nurse that had worked with them. He walked over and helped her gather up instruments, meeting her eye when she looked up at him. Turning to her, he tugged her mask down enough to see her face—to confirm what he already knew—then let it slip back up again.

"Nice job, Samantha."

"You too." He saw the admiration in her eyes.

"What are you doing here?" He couldn't keep the huskiness from his voice. Just the sight of her sharpened his senses.

"Carol didn't have anyone to send in to you. We had a cancellation, so I volunteered." She took off her mask and smiled at him.

"We'd have had a rough time without you. Thanks." His gaze dropped to her lips, and the memory of their kiss filled his mind.

It must have shown in his eyes because she took a step backward. "I uh, I'd better run. I just barely have time to grab a quick bite before office hours start."

He nodded.

"I'll look in on your patient in a few days if you don't mind. I'd like to meet him. And his family."

"Yeah, sure." He rested his hands at his waist. "Have you heard the weather prediction for this weekend? Sunny with highs near eighty. Indian summer."

She gave him a puzzled look, obviously surprised by this change of subject. "Yes, sounds great."

"I've got Sunday off. How about if you, Jonathan, and I . . ."

"No, Brad."

He breathed a discouraged sigh. "Come on, Samantha. Last weekend was a fluke. I had every reason to believe that I'd be free both those days, or I wouldn't have even attempted to make plans with Jonathan. These things happen occasionally."

"I know how often they happen, Brad."

"Doctors do manage to have personal lives, you know."

She met his gaze with a look of determination. "I know *exactly* the kind of personal lives doctors lead. I know it from a lifetime of experience. And I don't want to have to deal with it anymore. Don't want my son affected by it."

He studied her resolute expression. "Your father's hardly the typical physician, Samantha. The man's got more motivation and energy than anyone I've ever met. Much as I respect and admire him, I don't have that kind of drive."

The charge nurse interrupted them to tell Brad that his next case was ready. He acknowledged her, but his gaze remained on Samantha. "How about it, Sam? Jonathan would love the lake."

He saw her look of determination waver. She wanted to go. He could feel it.

"I'm sorry, Brad. No."

He watched her walk off and his jaw tightened in frustration.

Brad's suggestion continued to replay itself in Samantha's mind, however, and she came to a decision. *She* would take Jonathan to a nearby lake this weekend. She'd introduce her son to the advantages of this state that bordered on four of the five Great Lakes and also contained thousands of smaller ones.

She had in mind one that she'd particularly enjoyed as a child. Little White Fish Lake had a small, sandy beach and two floating, off-shore docks. She hoped it hadn't changed.

They left at ten o'clock on Saturday morning, and arrived a little over an hour later. Jonathan delighted in swimming out to the docks, and afterward they rented a small rubber raft with paddles and maneuvered around the lake. Upon returning to shore, they spread a blanket on the sand. As Samantha reclined upon it, enjoying what would likely be the last of the sun's summer-like rays, Jonathan became acquainted with another little boy. Together they played in the shallow water near the shoreline.

Keeping an eye on them, Samantha's thoughts drifted. Much as she and Jonathan had enjoyed themselves today, she wondered what it would have been like to have Brad share it with them. Jonathan would have loved it.

But then children didn't always know what was good for them.

On the way home, her son slept, deliciously exhausted by the physical activity. When Samantha carried him into the house, she breathed deeply the delightful aroma of his sun-drenched skin and the fresh air that permeated his clothing. It had been a delightful day and had refreshed her for the week of work ahead.

On Monday after work, as Samantha entered the house, she noticed Jonathan's jacket on a kitchen chair. He must have gotten home early and used the spare key they kept hidden under a flower pot to let himself in. She called out to him but received no answer. Then before she could call again, Samantha heard strangled sobs coming from the direction of Jonathan's bedroom.

Hurrying there, she found him lying face down on the bed, crying as if his heart would break. "Jonathan, honey, what's wrong?" She sat down on the edge of the bed and ran her hand soothingly over his back, but he didn't turn to her. His sobs shook him. He looked so small and vulnerable lying there. When Samantha tried to turn him to herself, he resisted, keeping his face determinedly to the wall. A feeling of alarm began to build. "Jonathan, please, tell me what's wrong. Did something happen at school today?" He nodded between sobs. "What happened? Please, tell me."

"The guys won't let me play softball with them." He gasped in a pained wail. "When they pick teams at school, nobody wants me."

"Why don't they want you, sweetheart?"

" 'Cause I'm no good!"

"Well, sure you are. You and Trevor played this summer."

Jonathan shook his head, but his sobs subsided a bit. "He's better than I am too. He's just nicer."

"But you're only learning. You'll get better."

"How can I get better if they won't let me play?" His words became a moan of frustration, and he began to cry again.

A feeling of impotence flooded Samantha. What could she do to help him? She knew almost nothing about the mechanics of baseball or softball. The boy's father had played with him, but Jonathan hadn't been much more than an infant then—just four years old when Kenneth died. And now his grandfather never had time for him. For just a moment, the possibility of seeking Brad's help entered her mind, but she rejected it. Best not to resurrect that relationship.

Watching Jonathan's shoulders shudder with sobs, however, she decided that she had to do something. "Do you want me to throw some balls to you? Maybe if you and I practice here at home, it will help."

He sat up slowly, drying his eyes on his sleeves and shrugging his shoulders.

"Sure, come on," she encouraged. "I'll change, and we'll go outside and give it a try."

Jonathan looked up at her through eyes that still brimmed with tears. "Do you know how to play softball?"

"Well, not exactly, but I can throw a ball. Get your equipment. I'll be ready in a minute."

Looking a little more hopeful, Jonathan went to his closet and took out his bat, ball, and glove. Samantha quickly changed into jeans and a sweatshirt and hurried to join him in the backyard.

She tossed a slow, easy ball towards his bat. He swung but missed. "It's okay, honey. Let's try a few more." She tossed two more balls, and he swung at and missed both of them.

"What am I doing wrong, Mom?"

"I'm not sure. I don't know much about this. But let's keep trying." After a few more throws, he finally hit one, but it only thudded awkwardly and rolled off his bat. "Watch the ball come towards you, Jonathan. I know you're supposed to watch the ball." She threw him several more, and he hit a couple of them, but none went more than a few feet.

"That's enough, Mom. Maybe we can try again later." He walked to the steps, leading to the screened-in back porch, and sunk onto the bottom one. Samantha sat next to him.

"If my Dad were here, he'd teach me."

"Yes, he would. He used to play ball with you, do you remember?"

"Sort of. I had my old red bat then."

"That's right, you do remember."

He nodded and poked the toe of his sneaker into the grass. "Why did he have to die, Mom?"

She put an arm around her son's shoulders and hugged him. "I don't know, sweetheart." The threat of tears stung the bridge of her nose, and choked her throat.

After a few moments, Jonathan rose from the step. "I think I'll try to find Mark," he told her, referring to a younger child in the neighborhood. He headed up the walkway towards the front of the house.

When he'd turned the corner, the tears slipped down Samantha's cheeks, and she wiped them away with the palms of her hands. She stood and went into the house. Maybe she could find out something about the techniques of softball at the library.

She went into her bedroom to hang up the uniform that she'd tossed on the bed earlier and then to the freezer to take out some meat for dinner. She also answered a worried telephone call from Jonathan's teacher, reassuring her that he'd gotten home safely. Afterward, Samantha ambled listlessly to the living room window, looking for Jonathan and wondering if he'd found Mark.

She saw him sitting alone on the curb in front of the house, his elbows resting on his knees and his chin in his hands. His blond tow-head turned occasionally as he watched the cars go by. He looked so small and forlorn, much younger than his six years. Samantha felt a stir of uneasiness: She shouldn't allow him to sit on the curb, but she hated to reprimand him right now.

Then suddenly her heart jumped to her throat as a vehicle approached uncomfortably close to the boy. Before she could move, however, she realized that it had come to a halt several feet from him. Starting for the front door, Samantha stopped as she recognized the dark green SUV and watched as Brad got out and walked over to her son.

Samantha observed their subsequent verbal exchange with mixed emotions. She didn't want any deepening of their relationship, but right now, talking to Brad might make Jonathan feel better. She moved to sit on the edge of a chair near the window from which she could watch them unnoticed.

Brad hunkered down to sit on the curb next to Jonathan. They talked in earnest for a few minutes, and then both got up. More accurately, Jonathan bounded up. He ran towards the backyard and soon returned, carrying his bat, ball, and glove. Handing the ball and glove to Brad, he gripped the bat with both hands and strode several feet away. Brad tossed him a few easy balls, and when Jonathan missed them, Brad stopped and seemed to instruct him.

As they talked, Samantha found herself watching Brad. He wore snug jeans and a dusty-blue, polo-style shirt, and she couldn't keep her gaze from traveling over his athletic build. With his wide shoulders and trim hips, one might mistake him for a professional athlete. He was better looking than ever, and suddenly the current situation seemed a cruel irony: After all her futile years of pining after him, now that he seemed interested in her, circumstances compelled her to avoid him.

She forced her attention back to their practice as Brad backed up and threw the ball again. This time when Jonathan swung at it, he hit it—further than he had with Samantha.

Brad stopped again and appeared to instruct Jon on the position of his feet. Then he stepped back and threw the ball once more. This time Jonathan hit it with a solid thwack. It flew towards the street, and for a moment, Samantha thought it might hit a passing car.

After retrieving the ball, the two conferred again, and then Jonathan came running towards the house. Samantha rose from her chair as he dashed in the front door, his face mirroring barely contained enthusiasm.

"Mom, Brad's going to take me to the park for batting practice." His words were not a request for permission; they were a declaration of intent. This was something new from her son: a resoluteness that she sensed would resist denial.

As much as she wanted to discourage their friendship, Jonathan's reversal from tears to determination was such a welcome relief that she acquiesced. Following him to the door as he raced out again, Samantha encountered Brad, waiting just outside. He eyed her warily.

"Okay, Brad. Let's go!" Jonathan was already halfway to the car.

Samantha gave Brad a weak but grateful smile. "I hope you can help him."

His mouth relaxed into the beginnings of a grin. "I think I can. He just needs to learn a few of the basics."

Her own mood lightened in response to this positive assessment, and optimism replaced worry. "I hope so. Thanks."

His dark eyes held hers. "Do you want to come along?"

The invitation came unexpectedly, and she started to shake her head. However, the thought of returning to the quiet house seemed dull compared with the allure of the park. Besides, maybe she could learn something that would help Jonathan later.

"Alright. Just let me get my keys and lock up the house."

As they drove to the park, Jonathan chattered ceaselessly, and Brad responded with good-natured ease. Once there, he helped Jonathan gather up his equipment, and they strolled out to a grassy field. Samantha settled on a gentle slope along the sidelines to watch.

Jonathan missed Brad's first two pitches, but after a few words of further instruction, he connected with a solid hit. Soon he was hitting the ball regularly, and Samantha smiled in astonished relief.

After they'd been playing for a while, Samantha noticed another boy watching from the sidelines. Following one of Jonathan's especially solid hits, the boy called out to him. "Hey, nice hit, Jon!"

Jonathan paused and waved to the boy, then he said something to Brad, who motioned for the other child to join them. Brad pitched a few balls to each one and then left them to pitch to each other and walked over to Samantha, chuckling under his breath.

She squinted up at him in the bright sunlight. "Why are you laughing? And who is that boy?"

Brad dropped down beside her and watched the boys for a few seconds before answering. "Jonathan called him Craig. Guess he's one of the kids at school that told Jon he wasn't good enough to play." He turned to smile at Samantha. "Jonathan listens to instructions and learns fast. He'll do all right with a little practice."

He lay back, propping himself on his elbows as they watched the youngsters warm to each other and then start in on good-natured horseplay.

Samantha experienced a wave of gratitude and reached out to touch Brad's arm. "Thank you, Brad."

He turned to her, and she suddenly realized how close he was. His dark eyes gazed into hers. "My pleasure."

When they turned back to watch the boys, Samantha saw that they now rolled on the ground, apparently wrestling with each other. Their antics appeared good-natured, but the other boy rapidly gained the upper hand, despite the fact that they were about the same size. Then as Craig pinned Jonathan's shoulders to the ground, Samantha started to rise, debating whether to interfere.

But she felt Brad's hand on her arm. "They're all right, Sam. Just horsing around."

She nodded and smiled. She guessed it took someone who had once been a boy to understand them. But she couldn't help turning back for another quick glimpse, and when she saw they'd gotten up and gone back to the bat and ball, her shoulders sagged in relief.

A moment later, she felt Brad's hand move over her back and turned to see a soft look in his eyes. "Those protective motherly instincts are really amazing, aren't they?"

She tossed her head. "I wasn't worried."

He chuckled. "Yeah, right."

Then a woman called to Craig from the other side of the field. After a few words to Jonathan, Craig ambled towards her, and Jonathan came bounding back to Brad and Samantha, covering the ground in long strides. "Craig had to go home. Will you pitch me some more balls, Brad?"

Samantha intervened. "We've got to go home now, Jonathan. It's almost dinner time, and your grandfather said he'd be home early tonight."

"Please, just for a little while?"

"We'll practice again soon, Jon." Brad got to his feet and reached out a hand to Samantha, pulling her up beside him. As they walked towards the car, he kept her hand lightly enfolded in his own, and she couldn't summon the will to pull it free.

Jonathan chattered most of the way home, and when they pulled up in front of the house, Samantha saw her father's car in the driveway. "Look, Grampa's home already."

Jonathan bounced up and down in the back seat. "I'm gonna tell him how good I hit the ball."

"How *well* you hit the ball," Samantha corrected.

"Yeah. You wanna have dinner with us, Brad?"

Brad brought the car to a halt and turned off the ignition. "I can't stay for dinner, but I'll come in for a few minutes and say hello to your grandfather."

"Are you sure you can't stay?" Samantha felt a sudden disappointment at the prospect of his leaving. "We're having chicken stir-fry, and it won't take long to prepare."

He stared at her for a moment, obviously surprised that she'd reinforced the invitation. "I can't tonight.

My parents are expecting me. But, I'd love to come another time."

In the living room, they found Dr. Howard, reclining in an easy chair, a drink in one hand and the newspaper in the other. This was one of his rare free evenings, and he apparently was luxuriating in it.

He turned as they entered, and his eyes brightened. "Brad, my boy! It's good to see you!" He raised his glass. "Have a drink with me?"

Brad extended his hand to shake the older man's, stepping to the chair so that Dr. Howard wouldn't have to rise. "No thank you, sir. I'm on duty again in a few hours."

Jonathan crawled up onto the arm of the chair. "Brad's teaching me to play softball, Grampa."

Dr. Howard patted Jonathan's knee and grinned broadly. "Well, I'd say you have an excellent instructor." He inclined his head towards Brad. "This young man was a remarkable athlete in high school. You never followed it up in college, though, did you, Brad?"

Brad shook his head. "No, sir, I had to work at my studies too hard. No time for athletics. I guess I've never been sorry though."

"No, no, of course not." Dr. Howard proceeded with uncharacteristic geniality. "You were right to concentrate your efforts where they'd produce the most return. You've become a fine surgeon."

Brad accepted the compliment with the nonchalance of one accustomed to hearing it. "Thank you, sir."

For the first time, Benton Howard addressed his daughter. "Yes sir, a fine surgeon. This young man's ambitious. He's going far."

His words caused something within Samantha to recoil, and as if Brad sensed this, he eyed her with furrowed brow. He spoke to Dr. Howard but continued watching the man's daughter. "I don't know if it's ambition so much as that I love the work."

Dr. Howard waved his drink in dismissal. "You remind me of myself at your age. Hard driving and aggressive."

Brad didn't contradict him again, but his eyes moved between the older man and Samantha. He shifted uneasily and glanced at his watch. "Gosh, I didn't realize it was getting so late. My parents are expecting me." As he rose and moved towards the front door, Samantha's father jumped to his feet. Slapping Brad on the back, he accompanied him outside, all the while chatting amiably.

Samantha watched the camaraderie, and couldn't help a wry smile. Perhaps she should have gone to medical school instead of into nursing. Maybe then her father would have taken more of an interest in her over the years.

But she could never remember a time when she'd wanted such an all-involving career. What she'd always wanted most was the close-knit family she'd never had. A loving husband and lots of babies.

And for a time, she'd had that, or was well on her way. Kenneth had been an attentive husband and a doting father. Jonathan and he had adored each other. Evenings and weekends always found Kenneth at home, engrossed in his family. They'd been happy.

Which proved it didn't take a grand passion to make a happy marriage. Kenneth had been almost ten years older than Samantha. He'd been a patient of hers, and they'd become friends. After a while, she'd learned to love him. He was a good and kind man, and she never regretted marrying him. When his heart attack took him from them, it broke her heart.

Dr. Howard returned to the house, and Samantha headed for the kitchen to prepare dinner. To her surprise, her father's buoyant mood continued throughout the meal, and he even asked Jonathan a few questions about school and softball. Finally, when they'd finished eating, he pushed back from the table as if to leave and then paused to smile almost shyly at his daughter and grandson.

"You know, it's kind of nice, having a relaxing evening to spend with my family." He spoke with a degree of self-consciousness and came as close to blushing as Samantha had ever seen. Then straightening suddenly, he became the self-assured professional again, slapping the table vigorously to punctuate his next words. "But now it's time to get back to my medical journals. I'm falling behind in my reading."

He disappeared in the direction of his den but a moment later reappeared. "By the way, Samantha, I called Josie today," he said, referring to the woman who had been his housekeeper for the first year after his wife's death but who now came in only once or twice a week to clean. "I asked her to come back and keep house for us full time." His voice took on a gruffer tone. "If you're going to insist on working for old Dwyer, I won't have you killing yourself trying to cook and clean around here too."

Samantha's mouth came close to dropping open at this uncharacteristic show of concern. "I appreciate that, Dad, but Jonathan and I will only be here for another month."

"Yes, well, we'll see about that."

She started to protest, but he headed for his den

again, and a moment later, she heard the door close behind him.

We'll see about that? He sounded as though he had something to say about it.

Well, he'd find out differently. She certainly didn't intend to alter their plans on the basis of one evening of congeniality.

Chapter Four

A few days later, Samantha stopped at the Farmer's Market on the way home from work to pick up some fresh sweet corn for dinner. As she sorted through the ears, placing the ones that appealed to her in a plastic bag, she heard a familiar voice.

"Samantha, dear! I almost didn't recognize you in your uniform."

Samantha turned to see Brad's mother. "Mrs. Davis! How nice to see you."

They chatted for a few moments, and the older woman asked about Samantha's job. Their friend, Ray Dwyer, couldn't say enough nice things about her, she said. Then Mary Davis reached out to touch Samantha's arm. "Oh, have you heard about Brad's offer?"

"From the medical group?" Samantha shook her head. "Is it official?"

"Oh yes. They want him to join them as soon as he's finished his residency next month." Her eyes danced as she spoke of her son. "The family's thrilled. Brad's worked so hard for so long. Now finally this type of situation will allow him to lead a slower-paced life. We'll all get to see much more of him."

"That's wonderful. Has Brad given them a definite answer then?"

"Not yet, but I'm sure he intends to soon." She frowned. "I'm surprised he hasn't told you. He seemed eager for you to know for some reason." A look of worry crossed her face. "Oh dear, maybe I wasn't supposed to say anything."

"When he tells me, I'll act surprised."

Mary gave Samantha a grateful smile, and then once again her eyes lit with enthusiasm. Samantha loved this about her: A perpetual air of happiness surrounded this woman. "I understand that Brad's been having some fun with Jonathan."

"Yes, he's helped him a time or two with batting practice so that Jon can compete with the kids at school. Brad's been great with him."

"Well, I'm sure that Bradley enjoys it too. He's very fond of Jonathan." She paused. "And so are we. If you ever need a sitter for him, please feel free to call on us." She smiled wistfully. "We don't see enough of our own grandchildren, and Jonathan is so like Trevor." She gave Samantha's arm a squeeze. "And I wish you'd come around more often too, dear. You know you've always been like a second daughter to us."

Samantha gave Mary a hug. "Thank you." Her voice caught, and they held each other for a moment.

Mary Davis had been a good friend of Samantha's mother, and they'd become especially close after their children had grown and gone. Samantha would have

loved Mary for that reason alone; however, Brad's
mother had many other endearing qualities. Outwardly
an extremely attractive woman, she also possessed an
inner warmth and kindness.

After she'd left, Samantha vowed she'd visit Mary
soon. Somehow being with her made Samantha miss
her own mother just a little less.

And then her mind went back to the news about
Brad. A slower-paced lifestyle, his mother had said.
The family would get to see more of him. If that kind
of position really appealed to Brad, then her father had
been wrong about him—about his extraordinary ambition. She couldn't help a smile of satisfaction.

Samantha arrived home later than usual and called
out to Jonathan as she entered the house. Receiving
no answer, she proceeded to the kitchen with her grocery bags and spotted a note on the table. The hand-
writing was obviously that of an adult.

> *Samantha,*
> *Jonathan called, asking for a little more help*
> *with batting practice. We've gone to the park.*
> *Back around five.*
>
> *Brad*

Samantha stared at the brief missive. Jonathan had
called Brad? She couldn't imagine him feeling so free
to interrupt Brad's busy schedule. Glancing at the
clock, she noted that it was already ten minutes to five.
The stop at the market had delayed her longer than
she'd realized.

After putting the groceries away, Samantha show-
ered and changed into jeans and a pullover. Then deciding to bring in the evening newspaper before

starting dinner, she wandered out to the front yard. She had just bent to retrieve the paper when a vehicle turned into the driveway. It was Brad's SUV, and as soon as he'd turned off the engine, Jonathan scrambled out, slamming the door loudly.

"Hey, Mom! Can we go for burgers with Brad?" He looked up at her hopefully. "He has to eat dinner anyway before he goes back to the hospital, and if we go too, you won't have to cook anything. Can we, Mom?"

Brad came up behind Jonathan with a mischievous gleam in his eye. "Come on, Mom. Be a sport."

She shrugged. "Okay, I guess so, but . . ." Her gaze settled on her son. "What's going on? You called Brad?"

"Yeah! Craig promised to pick me for his team at lunch time recess tomorrow. I have to do good, Mom!"

Brad winked at her. "Jonathan got some great hits today. We practiced throwing and catching too." He reached down to squeeze Jonathan's shoulder. "You'll do all right, Jon."

On the way to the restaurant, Jonathan talked about their practice session: He'd hit the ball so much better than ever before, and Brad always knew what he'd done wrong when he messed up.

While they ate, Samantha watched in amazement at the rapport that had developed between Jonathan and Brad. As they discussed ball-playing strategy and joked with one another, she saw genuine enthusiasm in Brad's eyes. He wasn't merely tolerating her son, he was having a good time too.

Then Brad's gaze met hers in evident amusement at something Jonathan had said, and when he smiled and winked, a warmth spread through her. It must have shown in her expression because his eyes kept coming back to her after that. At one point their gazes held for several moments until forced apart by the arrival of the waitress. "Does anyone want dessert?"

Jonathan asked for ice cream.

"And how about your mom and dad?"

Samantha felt her face color, but Brad merely flashed a devilish smile and told the waitress he'd pass. Samantha also declined.

When they arrived home, Jonathan raced to the den to tell his grandfather about their practice session, and Samantha turned to Brad. "Thank you for helping him. I know how little free time you have."

"It was fun. Jonathan's a great kid." But his mind obviously wasn't on the boy. He looked into her eyes, and then his gaze dropped to her lips. His large form loomed over her and the scent of his aftershave surrounded her. Almost unaware of what she was doing, Samantha took a step towards him. He reached for her, but suddenly Jonathan's footsteps come pounding back.

"Grampa said he'd like to come with us to the park sometime."

Samantha pulled her gaze from Brad's as Jonathan's words registered. Her father? Playing baseball with Jonathan and Brad? Was the world going mad?

Brad left soon after that. But not before he and Samantha shared a few more lingering gazes.

And later in bed that night, she couldn't stop thinking about him. Perhaps she needn't be quite so guarded about her feelings after all. He was about to accept a job that would allow him a maximum of free time for one in his profession. That fact alone went a long way towards answering her major reservations about him.

And more than once, he'd said in no uncertain terms that he had nowhere near her father's level of ambition or energy. She hadn't believed him at first, but mounting evidence suggested that he'd spoken the truth. Just look at all the time he'd spent with Jonathan lately.

Optimism started to build, but she forced a damper on it, reminding herself that he'd also canceled two planned outings with her son. *Take it slowly and see how things develop*, she told herself. *One step at a time.*

A few nights later on a Friday evening, Samantha drove down a street of obviously expensive homes. Pulling to the side of the road, she dug into her purse for the slip of paper on which she'd written the address. Upon consulting it, she slumped into her seat with a sigh of dismay. Sure enough, it was the house she'd just passed—with cars crowding not only the driveway but the street for half the block on either side. The home belonged to the charge nurse in surgery and her husband, a head honcho in administration at the hospital.

Carol Gregson had invited Samantha for what she described as a gathering of friends to help her celebrate her birthday, and Samantha had gotten the distinct impression that it was a small, hastily-arranged affair. Carol had told her to dress casually and also warned that anyone with a gift would be refused admittance.

The party had obviously turned into a large one, and Samantha now felt underdressed in her casual black slacks and gray knit top. And the small gift of fudge for Carol's sweet tooth, which she couldn't resist buying, now seemed pathetically insignificant.

She sighed again. She might as well go in. Returning home to change clothes would take too long and shopping for another gift at this late hour was out of the question. She pulled into the nearest parking place.

Carol answered the bell in jeans and a pullover, which eased Samantha's concern about her own dress. Carol was a few years older than Samantha, and with her short dark hair and trim figure, was attractive in an athletic, tomboyish fashion. She possessed a sense of humor that disarmed most people and a down-to-earth manner that put them at ease. Despite this, she managed to maintain the edge of authority needed to carry out her job.

Carol welcomed Samantha with enthusiasm, and once inside, introduced her to several vaguely familiar faces from the hospital. Samantha knew a few of the nurses from surgery and enjoyed becoming better acquainted with them. In addition, as the evening wore on, she found herself parrying the advances of a young resident.

The next couple of hours—filled with gift opening, off-key renditions of "Happy Birthday," and the cutting of the cake—passed quickly, and Samantha began to think about leaving. It had been a busy week, and a full day of chores awaited her tomorrow.

She looked around for Carol to tell her good-bye and spotted her at the door, opening it to a tardy arrival. When the tall, dark-haired man entered, Samantha's heart did a familiar flip. She'd wondered why he hadn't come, and as the evening wore on, assumed that he wouldn't or couldn't. But now, as Brad moved into the room, his presence seemed to give the gathering a new vitality. He said something to Carol, and they both laughed, then he joined a small group of people near the door.

Samantha tried to keep her mind on the conversation going on in her own circle, but the next time she glanced Brad's way, their gazes met. She started to smile just as an attractive brunette sidled up to him, her gaze playing with his flirtatiously. When the woman began fingering the lapel of Brad's sport jacket, Samantha turned away.

But she couldn't restrain her gaze for long, and the next time she looked, Brad was moving her way— without the brunette. A moment later, he stood next to her.

She deduced by his sport jacket and tie that he had come from the hospital. He'd apparently stopped to shave, however, because the familiar fragrance of his lotion floated around her and sent ripples of awareness along her nerve endings. Somehow, she managed a smile and a greeting.

Brad murmured a response, and his arm stole around her waist. An intensity that she hadn't seen before burned in his eyes.

Several people standing nearby greeted Brad, and as he bantered with them, Samantha studied him. His dark hair and eyes, combined with his six-foot plus frame gave him an air of virile masculinity. And his relaxed and easy manner implied a self-assurance one could only envy. Then her gaze came to rest on his lips, and her mind raced back to that day on the sofa, when he had kissed her. The sensations of that night stirred within her anew.

Then he turned to her again, and his eyes probed

hers gently. "I didn't expect you to be here, but I guess I should have realized you knew Carol."

Samantha nodded. "I didn't know it would be this big a party." She told him a little about the activities that had preceded his arrival, and as she spoke, his gaze dropped to her lips. His hand came up to caress her waist once more, and he drew her slowly towards himself.

But someone spoke to him again, and he turned to answer. However, his arm came up to encircle Samantha's shoulders and nestle her into his side, and she sensed that the gesture didn't go unnoticed by several of those present.

A few minutes later, a group of men beckoned to Brad from across the room. Excusing himself, he caught Samantha's hand, and he drew her along.

Moving towards the circle of young residents, Brad could feel the delicate bones of Samantha's fingers in his large hand. He'd seen the look in her eyes and knew he wasn't taking unwanted liberties by keeping her near him. He felt even more certain when her fingers intertwined with his own and clung.

He hoped every guy in the room was watching because his actions were a show of possession and that's exactly what he intended. He couldn't ever remember feeling this way about a woman before.

When they reached the new group, Brad introduced Samantha. They were younger residents wanting to pick Brad's brain, and he indulged them.

After some time, Brad's beeper went off. He excused himself to go to the telephone, and when he returned, whispered to Samantha that he had to get back to the hospital.

"Already? Are you on call?"

He shook his head and eyed her worriedly. Officially he was off duty. "But an elderly patient of mine is in critical condition. I asked them to call me if she worsened." His eyes pleaded for understanding. "She doesn't have any family, and I don't want her to . . . be alone."

Samantha wondered if he meant to die alone, but she didn't ask. "I'll walk out with you," she told him. "I never meant to stay this late. I have a busy day tomorrow." They sought Carol out to thank her for the party.

Brad walked Samantha to her car. "I'm sorry I have to leave. I would have liked to spend more time with you."

"I would have liked that too. Maybe another time."

He started to nod and then paused. His brow furrowed in thought. "How about Sunday?"

"Sunday?"

"Carol and Jim have invited me to go sailing on Lake Michigan. I know they wouldn't mind if I brought a guest along. They're always urging me to." He gave her a cajoling look. "It's supposed to be a beautiful day. Maybe the last of Indian summer before fall sets in."

The hope that he was different from her father warred with lingering doubts. But the words escaped her lips before she could stop them. "That sounds like fun. I'd like to go."

Brad smiled and nodded. "I'll call you tomorrow about the time." He opened the car door for her, and she got in. When he bent to the window to say goodnight, she thought for a moment he might kiss her, but he straightened and stepped away from the car, lifting a hand in farewell.

Driving home, Samantha couldn't help wondering if she'd done the right thing by accepting his invitation. Then something he'd said the night they'd kissed came back to her: "Wait until you know me better and then judge me as an individual." How could she do that if she didn't spend time with him? She smiled in anticipation of Sunday.

The next morning, Samantha spoke with her father about the possibility of his minding Jonathan on Sunday so that she could go sailing with Brad. Dr. Howard informed her, however, that he already had other plans. He was leaving for Detroit early the next afternoon to attend a medical convention and would be gone until Tuesday evening. He reminded her, though, that Josie planned to begin working for them full time on Monday. Perhaps she could come a day early and care for Jonathan. Samantha tried unsuccessfully to reach her several times during the day.

She was preparing to call Brad to explain the situation when she passed a window and saw her son talking to both Brad and Mary in the Davises' front yard. Samantha hurried outside.

Brad's mother saw her first. She'd obviously been gardening because she wore a straw hat and fabric gloves. "I hope you don't mind my borrowing Jonathan for a while. He's such a good worker." A few feet away, Jonathan struggled to empty a bucket of weeds into a large container near the house.

"I'm glad that he wants to help."

"Can you be ready to go tomorrow morning at about eight o'clock?" Brad asked. "It's almost a two-hour drive to the marina, and Jim and Carol like to get out on the lake as early as possible."

Samantha gave him a disheartened look. "I may not be able to go after all." She proceeded to explain the situation and had not quite finished when Mary Davis interrupted.

"Of course you can go! Jonathan will stay with me, won't you, Jonathan?"

The boy nodded enthusiastically. "I can help Mrs. Davis with the gardening again."

"Or maybe we could drive over and see Trevor."

"Yeah! Let's go see Trevor!"

"Oh, Mrs. Davis, that would be great. But are you sure? We'd probably be gone most of the day."

"I'm absolutely certain. You just plan to go and have a good time." She cast a look of motherly concern at her son. "And keep Brad's mind off his work for a few hours."

Samantha smiled up at Brad. "I guess I can go after all."

"Thanks, Mom. You're great." He gave his mother a hug.

Samantha and Brad agreed to meet the following morning at the Davis house.

Both Samantha and Jonathan rose early. After combing her hair into a ponytail, Samantha donned white jeans and a navy T-shirt. Then stuffing her one-piece swimsuit into an oversized purse, she grabbed a beach towel and her red jacket—in case the wind turned cool out on the water—and headed for the kitchen.

Excitement rippled through her at the prospect of the day's outing. She'd gone sailing only once or twice before and had loved every minute of it. And the anticipation of spending an entire day with Brad, uninterrupted by calls from the hospital, filled her with a nervous delight.

She reached the kitchen to find that Jonathan had already fixed himself a bowl of cold cereal. A short while later, he stood dressed and ready to go—fifteen minutes early and with several toys in tow to take to Trevor's house.

They arrived next door shortly before eight o'clock. Brad had gotten there a few minutes earlier, so Samantha bade Jonathan a hasty good-bye, and gave Mary a hug of appreciation.

Moments later, they were on the road. With the sun shining and the air warm, they left the car windows open for most of the two-hour drive to Lake Michigan, arriving at the marina shortly before ten o'clock.

As Brad pulled the SUV into the near-empty parking lot, Samantha looked out over the mast-filled cove. The sun glistened on the rippling water, and the boats rocked in a gentle current. A wooden dock stretched before them, between the water and an oblong patch of green grass, which contained a picnic table and an oval flower garden.

They climbed out of the Jeep and immediately spotted Carol and Jim, waving to them from the deck of their sailboat. Gathering up their extra clothing and towels, they each grasped a handle of the drink-filled cooler that Brad had brought and struck out onto the wooden dock.

Carol and Jim greeted them cheerfully and with undisguised pride, accepted Samantha's compliments on their boat, which Brad had referred to as a "sloop." The brass railings gleamed in the sunlight and the wood-grained cabin shone with a high gloss.

After stowing the cooler below, they prepared to set

out. Carol and Samantha settled onto bench-like seats along one side of the craft while the men prepared to get under way.

They maneuvered out of the boat slip and proceeded through a narrow channel, waving to passengers in other boats and passing a red lighthouse. Brad and Jim had obviously piloted the boat together before, because they moved with practiced precision.

Soon they had moved out upon the open waters of Lake Michigan, and as the swifter breezes caught the sails, their speed increased. The wind, which tugged at their jackets and whipped through their hair, felt invigorating but not uncomfortably cool.

Samantha couldn't keep her gaze from Brad as he moved about the boat. He wore tan shorts and a yellow polo-style shirt, and the wind ruffled his thick, dark hair. As he laughed and bantered with Jim, she experienced a sensation of unreality. Could she really be out here in this beautiful place with Brad? The same Brad she'd pined over and dreamed about for most of her adolescent and teen years?

When they were well out on the open water, Brad came and dropped down on the seat beside Samantha. As they sailed along, he spotted a school of fish and leaned over to point them out to her. When he settled back again, his arm remained behind her in the semblance of a loose embrace, and she had to resist the impulse to snuggle in closer.

After a while, the mildly buffeting breeze and the gently snapping sails lulled her into a delicious repose, and she did relax against him. His hand dropped down to caress her shoulder for a moment, before returning to the back of the seat.

They sailed for over an hour, occasionally passing

other sailing craft. They glided past rows of beach houses, some large and spacious and others modest, but most with people milling nearby and walking on adjacent beaches. Everyone seemed intent on taking advantage of this last gasp of summer.

After a while, the distance between shoreline homes increased, and soon they were passing a series of isolated beaches. Even the number of passing boats dwindled to an occasional one in the distance or along the horizon.

Then a small isolated cove with a tiny marina came into view, and Brad rose to help Jim guide the sloop towards it. Several of the slots stood vacant, including one that belonged to a friend of Jim's, who had already taken his own boat out of the water for the season. They maneuvered into it and tied up.

"There's a great little beach about a quarter of a mile down this way," Jim told them, pointing along the shoreline. "We thought it'd be fun to picnic and swim there."

They changed into their suits, then gathered up blankets, jackets, cooler, and the sandwiches that Carol had brought, and struck out on the short hike. Exiting a wooden dock, they passed a boathouse and an old General Store, before heading out onto the sand.

After plodding along the hard-packed shoreline for about fifteen minutes, they arrived at an area at the base of a large sand dune. Two smaller dunes on either side helped to form a protective cove. Jim and Brad stopped and set down the cooler. "If we spread our blanket here, we'll be protected if the breeze turns cool and yet we're still right on the water," Jim told them.

"Isn't this great?" He waved his hands to indicate the general surroundings. "It's one of our favorite spots."

Looking out over the natural artistry of the seascape, they all agreed it was beautiful. The huge expanse of blue-green lake blended with the deep azure of the sky at an almost indiscernible horizon. Here and there an occasional white gull soared and dipped through the air. And nearby a succession of curling waves crashed onto the shore, churning up a sandy foam.

"Not another soul in sight," Carol added. "Most of the summer people have gone for the season and left us with our own little paradise. We came out here last weekend too."

They spread the blankets, placing several of the parcels they'd carried at the corners to secure them against the buffeting breeze. Then one by one they straggled towards the water's edge, digging their feet into the sand and letting the foam of the crashing waves wash over them.

The chilliness of the water tingled their toes at first, but they soon became accustomed enough to wade in deeper. As they did so, the water level rose to their knees, then to mid-thighs, and finally splashed onto their swimsuits. Samantha gasped as one particularly large swell sloshed up past her waistline. "I think this is far enough for me," she laughed.

"You mean you're not going to swim?" She couldn't tell whether or not Brad was teasing. "This water doesn't get much warmer, even during the summer." He snatched her hand and moved as if to tug her deeper.

Samantha struggled to pull free. "No don't, Brad!" Anxiety flashed in her eyes. "I hate cold water!"

Seeing her expression, Brad's teasing instincts fled.

He allowed her to retract her arm, but he came with it, until he stood directly in front of her. As he looked down into startled blue eyes, his hands, almost of their own accord, came up to rest at her slender waist. "Chicken," he mumbled, in an effort to hide tumultuous feelings.

Her hands moved to his upper arms. "Let's go back up on the beach," she cajoled. Her face was just inches from his own, and he had to fight an impulse to kiss her. Releasing her, he took her hand again, and they waded back to the beach.

Samantha dropped down on the blanket beside Carol just as Jim issued a challenge. "C'mon, Brad, I'll race you out to the buoy!"

Brad eyebrows flew up in mock horror. "Are you kidding? That water's cold!"

Samantha picked up a handful of sand and flung it at his ankles. "Why, you phony!"

Brad laughed, but then turned and dashed into the water, getting a head start on Jim. Jim bounded after him, and soon both men were propelling themselves forward with long, powerful strokes. Carol and Samantha shouted encouragement.

As the two heads bobbed out into the distance, Samantha turned to encounter an amused expression on Carol's face. "What?" she asked.

Carol's mouth curved into a leering grin. "Wow! You and Brad."

"What about us?"

"I don't think I've ever seen him look at a woman like that before. He actually looks smitten."

Samantha dug her feet into the sand and hugged her knees. "You're exaggerating."

"We've been trying all summer to get him to bring

a date out here, but he always said there was no one he cared to ask." She smiled slyly. "I guess he finally found someone."

"It's just a casual date."

"Uh-huh."

The men reached the buoy and then headed back. As they neared shore, the women stood for a better view of the race's end. Brad reached the shallow water first, and splashed through it as he bounded onto the sand. He made his way towards Samantha, and a moment later, stood in front of her, grinning and breathing heavily with exertion.

"Congratulations." She smiled up at him. Their gazes held, and his grin faded as he dipped his head and touched her lips with his own. Walking back towards the blanket, Samantha avoided Carol's gaze, knowing the smirk that surely lingered on her face.

Brad and Jim spread large towels on either side of the blankets, and lay down to absorb the sun's drying rays.

"I guess Brad won," Carol said.

"I gave him a head start coming back."

Brad guffawed, and the two men argued and kidded each other before falling silent and basking in the warm sun.

"You know what would taste good?" Carol's voice broke the silence. "Some of those barbecue potato chips with our sandwiches."

Jim moaned. "You don't need chips. They're loaded with fat."

"They might have the low-fat ones. C'mon. Let's walk back to the store."

Jim groaned again. "I knew that was coming."

Carol slapped him playfully on the thigh. "C'mon,

lazy. The exercise will do you good." She turned to Samantha and Brad. "You guys want to come?"

Brad chuckled. "No thanks. I'm just the friend. I don't have to cater to your whims."

Carol bounded up. "Okay, but don't expect any of my chips." She pulled her grumbling husband to his feet, and they headed back towards the marina and the General Store.

Chapter Five

"**Y**ou didn't volunteer to go with them. Don't you like chips?" Brad sat up next to Samantha. She wobbled her hand to indicate a so-so opinion, and let his gaze hold hers. "Darn," he gave a slow, provocative grin. "I was hoping you'd stayed behind just to be with me."

His nearness took her breath away, but she kept her voice steady. "Actually, I lied," she told him. "I love chips."

His smile broadened and then faded, then his head dipped to touch her lips again with his own. He pulled back to look into her eyes, but a moment later, his mouth descended to cover hers once more, this time more coaxingly. His third kiss increased in urgency, and Brad slipped a hand to the back of Samantha's neck to pull her mouth more firmly against his own. A yearning built with head-spinning rapidity, and Samantha dipped her head away.

Brad released her, and they sat looking out at the gently surging waves for several moments before he spoke again. "There's something I've been wanting to tell you."

She turned to him. "What's that?"

"I've pretty much decided to take the position with that group I told you about."

"That's great, Brad. Have you given them a definite answer?"

He paused and looked out at the water again. "No. Not yet."

Samantha studied his expression. Somehow he didn't seem as enthused as she would have expected. Perhaps he still had some details to iron out. "Your family must be happy about it." She felt a little guilty pretending ignorance.

"Yeah. They're looking forward to my having a little more free time." He turned to her, and his gaze seemed to travel over her facial features; then he smiled. He was looking at her but not into her eyes, and she became self-conscious.

"What?" she asked.

His grin widened. "The sun's bringing out your freckles."

"Oh no," she groaned, covering her face. "Don't look. I hate them."

"They're beautiful," he whispered and leaned towards her again, nuzzling her ear. She felt his warm breath, and it seemed so natural to turn to him. His mouth was warm and his kiss possessive, and she couldn't help responding.

But when their kisses once more became heated, she dropped her head and leaned away, then pulled herself to her feet. "That water looks nice."

She walked towards the waves, and Brad watched her go, willing himself not to follow. He'd better slow down. Samantha still had doubts. He watched her wade out almost to her waist before turning back. When she returned to shallow water, she looked over at him and smiled. "Doesn't feel quite so chilly now."

Brad rose to his feet and moved towards her; he couldn't help himself. He paused before her, drinking her in, his emotions churning. "Do you know how beautiful you are?" he murmured.

She grinned, squinting in the sunlight. "Even with freckles?"

"Especially with freckles."

His gaze moved to the horizon before returning to her. "Samantha, I uh . . . I'd like for us to see a little more of each other. Get to know each other better. How does that sound to you?"

The teasing glint remained in her eyes. "So knowing each other practically since birth hasn't done it?"

"I'm talking about the adult 'us'." He laughed and shook his head. "You don't plan to make this easy, do you?"

"I'm sorry." The glint faded from her eyes, and her smile turned warm. "I think seeing more of each other sounds very nice."

"Good." He looked out at the horizon again and then back at her. "Know what?"

"What?"

"I think you're going to have to move away one more time or I'm going to kiss you again."

She took a single step backwards. "I don't know how long I can keep doing this."

Brad gave a soft moan, then capturing her face in

his hands, lowered his mouth to hers—just as a shrill whistle rang out.

"Hey you two! Behave yourselves!" Jim grinned at them from a short distance away and Carol waved her bag of chips.

When they drew near, Jim paused to stand in front of Brad, studying him, and his grin widened. "You're right, Carol," he told his wife with a wiggle of his eyebrows, "Brad looks plum smitten."

"Shut up, smart guy."

"Told you," Carol smirked.

They moved to the blankets, and Carol flopped down. "All right, gang, let's break out the sandwiches. I'm starved! And if you're all really nice to me, I might share a few of my chips."

After lunch they threw a Frisbee around, and as the afternoon wore on, the air became noticeably cooler. Shivering in a chilly breeze, they packed up and trudged to the marina. On the trip back, with the water choppier than before, Brad and Jim kept busy maintaining the boat on course.

At their home marina, they helped the Gregsons tidy up the boat. Then thanking them for an enjoyable day, Samantha and Brad started for home. As the car entered the freeway, Samantha leaned her head back against the seat. "That was a fantastic day, but I'm exhausted."

"Go ahead and sleep. I'll wake you when we get home."

"Who will keep you awake?"

He smiled. "You forget, staying awake when I'm tired is what I do these days."

After a few minutes, she rolled her head his way.

"Tell me about the group you're planning to join. Where are their offices located?"

As Samantha listened to Brad describe the details, she studied his expression. Once again, he didn't seem as enthused as she might have expected. He was, after all, talking about the situation in which he would likely spend the rest of his professional life.

"Aren't you excited about the job, Brad?"

He threw a quick glance her way. "Yeah, sure. Why?"

"I don't hear any enthusiasm in your voice when you talk about it."

"I have something else on my mind right now." He reached for her hand. "I should have a night off towards the end of the week. Will you have dinner with me?"

"I'd like that."

He threw her another quick glance and a smile before forcing his eyes back to the heavy traffic. "I'll call you as soon as I know whether it's Friday or Saturday."

After she'd tucked Jonathan into bed that night, Samantha sat in the living room, trying to concentrate on the newspaper that she hadn't had time to read that morning. She failed after several attempts, however, and finally gave up.

Curling into the corner of the sofa, she gave herself up to thinking about Brad. A mixture of excitement and warm contentment suffused her as she mentally relived the day's experiences. The more she came to know Brad, the more she respected and trusted him.

Then tired from the long day, Samantha decided to take a warm shower and go to bed early. She'd have

to get up at the crack of dawn because Josie was starting full-time with them tomorrow. She'd agreed to arrive early to go over the details of her duties before
Samantha left for work.

Locking all the doors and turning out the lights,
Samantha headed for her bedroom. Somehow the
house seemed eerily quiet tonight. Surely it couldn't
be because of her father's absence. She'd never become accustomed enough to his presence to miss him.
Ah well, she yawned, at any rate, he would return
from his medical convention the day after tomorrow.

Brad pulled the mask from his nose and mouth as
he exited the operating room. Ten o'clock and he was
bushed. He hoped he could get away before another
emergency came in.

Apart from the four hours of sleep he'd gotten the
night before, he'd been at the hospital every waking
hour for the past two days. He paused at a hallway
window to gaze out at the rain-soaked night just as a
bolt of lightning lit the sky. Didn't look like the storm
had abated much.

He turned back to the dimly-lit corridors. They were
quiet now, the day's scheduled surgical cases having
been finished up hours ago. Walking towards the doctor's lounge to change into his street clothes, he passed
the orthopedic wing and saw a flurry of activity going
on in one of the operating rooms there: Both doctors
and nurses hurried in and out.

Down another corridor, Brad noticed the night
nurse, filling in the details of that emergency on the
scheduling board, and he ambled over to investigate.
As he read the entry, he stared in shock, unable to

react for a moment. Then wheeling around, he raced towards the orthopedic wing.

Samantha winced as lightning lit the sky and thunder crashed loudly. Then letting the drapes of her bedroom window fall closed, she padded back to bed and nestled in against the stacked pillows. She hoped Jonathan was sleeping deeply enough now so that the storm wouldn't wake him again. Pulling the covers up over herself, she reached for her book and tried to ignore the torrents of rain that pelted the roof.

Usually she enjoyed a good storm, but the violence of this one unsettled her. The lightning and thunder had been rolling in almost constantly for over two hours, and heavy rain had been falling since she and Jonathan arrived home from school and work that afternoon.

Samantha glanced at the clock. Eleven-thirty. She wondered if her father had decided to remain in Detroit for the night rather than drive in the storm. "You'd think he'd have enough consideration to call if he weren't coming," she mumbled. But then again, maybe the weather had just slowed his progress.

She snuggled more deeply into her pillows and was just becoming engrossed in her book when the doorbell rang. *Good, he was home.* He'd probably forgotten his key. Stepping into her slippers, she pulled on her robe and hurried to the front door.

When she opened it, Brad stood gazing down at her. "Brad! What are you doing here this time of night?" Then she noticed his somber expression. "What's wrong?"

"May I come in?"

"Yes, of course." She stepped aside.

He closed the door behind himself, then turned to face her, gripping her shoulders with his large hands. "Samantha, honey, your father's had an automobile accident."

She stared at him, and cold fear spread through her. Her mind raced with questions she was afraid to ask.

"His injuries don't appear to be life threatening, sweetheart. And there don't seem to be any internal injuries. But he does have some broken bones and a mild concussion. He's in surgery now."

She searched his face. "Surgery?"

"His car was hit broadside . . . on the driver's side. He has a broken pelvis and two compound fractures of his lower left leg—both the tibia and fibula."

Samantha hands flew to her mouth. "Oh, God."

Brad's arms came around her, and he cradled her against himself. "It doesn't look serious, sweetheart. He'll be all right."

"I'd better go to him." She struggled to think rationally. "But I can't leave Jonathan."

"My mother's on her way over. She'll stay with him. You go and get dressed. I'll take you to the hospital."

Samantha nodded, still dazed, and hurried to her bedroom. She pulled on jeans and a sweater, and by the time she got back to the foyer, Mary Davis had arrived. For some reason when Samantha saw her, her eyes flooded with tears.

Mary embraced her. "He's going to be all right, Samantha. Just keep telling yourself that." Then releasing her, Mary spoke calmly. "Go to your father, and don't worry about anything here. I'll stay with Jonathan for as long as you need me."

Samantha wiped away her tears and nodded, then

slipped into the raincoat Brad held open for her. They hurried out to his car, Brad holding an umbrella over their heads.

Moving along the darkened streets with the windshield wipers whipping back and forth at top speed, Samantha's mind began to function. *Please, please let him be all right*, she prayed. She couldn't bear the thought of losing another member of her family.

They stopped for a red light, and Brad reached over and took her hand. "They're only broken bones, Samantha."

"How bad is the concussion?"

She heard the pause before he answered. "They're pretty sure it's a mild one."

The light changed, and they continued on. Samantha flinched as lightning split the darkness, revealing the hospital, which loomed before them. It appeared dark and forboding, and she felt suddenly afraid to face the situation inside.

Brad ushered her into the building, then into an elevator, and finally down a corridor to the waiting room outside surgery. He helped her out of her wet coat, and after shedding his own, went to the telephone on a nearby table. He punched two buttons. "This is Brad Davis. Is Doctor Howard still in surgery?" He listened for what seemed an eternity. "Okay, thanks Jan. Look, I'm in the waiting room with his daughter. Will you let us know when they're finished?"

Samantha's eyes remained riveted on Brad's face as he replaced the receiver, trying to read his expression. "They've finished pinning his hip, Sam. They're working on his lower leg now. Jan thinks they'll be finished in half an hour."

When he sat down next to her and took her hands

again, she squeezed his tightly. "Will you go in there, Brad? See how he's doing and come back and tell me?"

"I can't go in street clothes, Samantha."

"Stay in the hall then. Tap on the window. Someone will come out and tell you."

"You know I shouldn't even do that. Besides, I don't want to leave you alone."

"I'll be all right, Brad. Please."

He gave a resigned sigh. "Promise you'll wait right here."

"I promise."

After he'd left, Samantha paced the room. How could this be happening? Why did she keep losing the people she loved? First her mother, then Kenneth, and now her father. True, she and her father had never been close, but she did love him, despite everything. Samantha realized that she hadn't acknowledged that fact, even to herself, for a long time. Guilt and panic built, and she struggled to clamp a lid on her feelings.

She had to stop assuming that she would lose him. Only broken bones, Brad had said. She had to hold on to that.

Samantha walked to the window and stared at the large drops of water that streamed in horizontal rivulets across the glass. She *did* have some vaguely pleasant memories from early childhood and the feeling that she and her father had once been close. But since adolescence, her resentment toward him had grown. It had reached its high point with her mother's death, and she had left. Since her return to Glen Arbor, she'd treated her father with coolness. Had she been justified? And could she forgive herself if she lost him now? She leaned her forehead against the cool glass.

"They've finished, Samantha." She spun around at the sound of Brad's voice. "They're taking him to ICU."

She saw in his eyes the guarded look of a professional and braced herself. "Is he all right?"

"He had a couple episodes of irregular heartbeat during the surgery. He's stabilized now, but they're keeping a close eye on him."

His heart? Fear tightened her chest as memories of Kenneth's death flooded back. Her husband had gone so fast. She quashed the building terror. Fate wouldn't be so cruel as to deal her the same blow a second time.

"Can I see him?"

He nodded, watching her with concern. "I'll go with you."

Brad retrieved both their coats and wrapped his free arm around her. As they made their way to the elevator and then down to the fifth floor, that arm sustained her and held her worst fears at bay.

They entered the Intensive Care Unit and saw him in a bed at the far end of the room. He lay with his eyes closed, looking deathly pale. The surgical intubation tube still protruded from his mouth and throat, keeping his air passages open, and an electrocardiogram machine monitored his heartbeat. A plastic bag of IV fluid hung from a nearby stand, dripping its contents into his left arm.

Slowly, Samantha approached. She'd never seen him look anything but robust and healthy before. Indeed, she'd rarely even seen him asleep. A wave of nausea rose in her throat.

She looked up at Brad, and saw his jaw tense in understanding. "You see it every day, but it's different when it's someone you love." His arm tightened around her shoulders. "But he's doing fine, Samantha." He inclined his head towards the cardiogram screen. "He's holding steady."

She nodded.

Then suddenly her father moved and gagged, and Brad snatched the intubation tube from his throat. Benton Howard's eyes fluttered open and stared unseeingly for a moment, finally coming to settle on Samantha.

She saw his confused and questioning look and stepped closer, touching his arm. "You had an accident, Dad. But you're going to be fine." Frown lines appeared on his brow, then disappeared as he slipped back into unconsciousness.

Samantha wasn't sure how long she stood staring down at him, before she felt Brad's hands on her shoulders again. "We can stay with him, Sam, but come and sit down." She let him guide her to a chair a few feet from the bed. Then he disappeared for a moment and returned with a chair for himself, which he placed next to hers. They settled into a silent vigil, interrupted only by the ICU nurse's frequent checks on Dr. Howard's blood pressure and other vital signs.

In the quiet of the night, Samantha's mind again drifted back over the years. So much time. So many countless hours they could have spent together and didn't. In many ways, they hardly knew each other.

And yet, the unexpected realization came to her that even in his frequent and protracted absences, she had felt his impersonal, detached brand of love and concern for her mother and herself. Even while obscure driving forces compelled him to strive and succeed—

well past the point of professional duty or provision for his family's needs—she'd sensed his caring.

She studied his pale features and prayed that they would yet get the opportunity to establish some sort of understanding between them. She let her head fall back against the back of the chair, and after awhile, drifted off.

She woke with a start to the sight of Brad, standing now and staring out the window. When she stirred, he turned to her and smiled. "The rain's stopped."

For the first time since he appeared at her door last night, Samantha noticed the dark smudges around his eyes, and the fact that his shoulders sagged with fatigue. She looked at her watch: three A.M. She sat up. "Go and get some sleep, Brad. You have to work tomorrow. I'll be all right now."

He shook his head. "I got someone to cover for me."

"But you'll have to make up the time, eventually. Please, sleep while you can."

He straightened and shoved his hands into his pockets. "I'm staying, Samantha. Don't worry about me."

They turned to see one of the orthopedic surgeons approach. He snatched up the chart at the foot of Dr. Howard's bed and perused it quickly, nodding in satisfaction. He acknowledged Brad and extended a hand to Samantha. "You must be Benton's daughter. I'm Don Edwards."

"Yes, I know, Doctor. Samantha Richards."

He gave her a reassuring smile. "Your father seems to be doing pretty well. I'm going to send him down to a private room now."

Samantha glanced at the heart monitor. "His irregular heartbeat?"

"Seems steady, but we'll continue to monitor it."

He looked from Samantha to Brad. "You both look beat. Why don't you go home and get some sleep. There's nothing you can do here, and we'll keep you informed if there are any changes."

Samantha wanted to stay, but she knew that Brad wouldn't leave unless she did, and he needed his rest. No telling when he'd slept last. After accompanying her father to his room and seeing him settled, they left the hospital.

Back at the house, they found Brad's mother asleep on the sofa. The sound of the door closing woke her, however, and her eyelids fluttered open. She sat up, immediately alert. "How is he?"

"He's doing well," Brad told her. "So well that they kicked us out. Told us to get some sleep."

"That's wise. You both look tired."

"Thank you for staying with Jonathan, Mrs. Davis."

"You're welcome, dear. But why don't I stay the rest of the night. You can sleep in, and I'll get Jonathan off to school, and explain things to Josie when she gets here."

Samantha started to protest but didn't want to appear ungrateful. "Thank you. That's kind of you."

Mary also eyed her son with concern. "I hope you'll get some sleep too, Brad."

"I will, Mom."

Brad reached over to cup Samantha's chin. "Don't worry, huh? He's doing fine."

She gazed up at him and nodded. "Thank you for everything, Brad. I don't know what I'd have done without you."

His eyes softened, and his lips came down to touch hers.

"Take care of her, Mom," he admonished softly, his gaze never leaving Samantha.

"I will, honey. And *you* take care of *yourself.*"

He bent to kiss his mother's cheek. "You bet. G'night."

Chapter Six

At nine o'clock the following morning, after a hurried breakfast and a call to Maggie, explaining the
situation, Samantha headed for the hospital.

When she entered her father's room, he lay wide
awake with the head of his bed elevated and a half-
eaten tray of liquids on his bedside stand. Upon first
seeing her, he appeared embarrassed, then grimaced in
disgust. "A fine mess, huh?"

She gave him a wan smile. "These things happen.
Thank God it wasn't more serious."

He turned his head to gaze out the window. "Blasted
rain has finally stopped."

"Yes, it was a terrible storm."

"I should have stayed in Detroit until this morning."

She shrugged. "Hindsight."

"Patty stopped in a while ago," he said, referring to
his receptionist and office manager. "She's going to
cancel my appointments and get someone to handle

my emergencies for the next few days." He spoke almost emotionlessly, and Samantha knew he felt disheartened. "I'll have to get someone to take over the office temporarily. They tell me it'll be months before I can work again."

She sank into the chair at his bedside. "Of course it will, Dad. You've got some mending to do. And maybe you should give yourself another day or two before worrying any more about your practice."

"I can't stop worrying about it!" His eyes suddenly burned with frustration and anger. "Darn it, Samantha! Why did this have to happen?"

"It was an accident, Dad. Accidents happen." It felt strange consoling him. Strange that he needed consolation. He'd never needed *anything* from her before.

She also realized that she wasn't altogether comfortable conversing with him. They'd never talked much, other than to convey necessary information. Certainly not about their feelings. But people conversed with strangers. How ridiculous to feel uncomfortable with one's own father.

For the first time she noticed a black and blue discoloration near his temple. "Does that bruise on your forehead hurt?"

He reached up to touch it gingerly. "Not compared to everything else." He glared at his leg with disgust.

"Do you remember what happened?"

He shook his head. "Not much. I had just gotten off the freeway. The light at the junction of the exit ramp and Maple was green so I hurried to get through it. That's all I remember." He closed his eyes wearily. "They tell me some idiot skidded through a red light."

After a brief silence, his eyes fluttered open again. "Everything okay at home?"

"Yes. Fine. Except that we've been worried about you, of course."

"Did Josie start on Monday?"

"She did, and I think she'll work out fine. Please stop worrying. We can certainly handle things at home." She tried to think of something to distract and cheer him. "Jonathan would like to come and see you after school today. I think he needs to reassure himself that you're all right."

"Sure. Sure." He still sounded more troubled than pleased. His eyes closed again, and though they fluttered open once or twice, his breathing soon became rhythmic, and Samantha knew he'd drifted off to sleep.

The next week passed without any setbacks. Although his ordeal was not without pain, Benton Howard improved steadily, being both a healthy and a strong-willed man. By telephone, he kept tabs on his medical practice and saw to it that the emergency needs of his patients were met.

And Samantha adjusted to the additional demands placed upon her. Her routine consisted of running from her job, to visits with her father, then home to Jonathan at the end of the day. She didn't know what she'd have done without Josie. Since she did the cooking and most of the cleaning now, Samantha could relax for at least a little while when she came home from work.

In the evenings, she'd sometimes take Jon to visit his grandfather and was surprised to find they delighted in each other's company. Jonathan would chatter on about his day at school, and once or twice he even took some of his textbooks and worksheets to show his grandfather.

And Brad became a significant source of emotional support, especially during those early days following the accident, stopping by both Benton's hospital room and the Howard home frequently.

Towards the end of the first week of Dr. Howard's hospitalization, Samantha received a telephone call. The manager of the condominium complex told her that their unit would be available in just two weeks.

Explaining her predicament, Samantha asked if they could hold the place until she knew how long her father would need care after returning home. Although sympathetic, the manager explained that they could not hold it. However, she told Samantha of another unit that would become available soon after the first of the year. Samantha assured her they would definitely be ready to move by that time.

Then ten days after the accident, Benton Howard came home. Knowing that his condition would confine him to bed for a while, he'd hired a practical nurse to come in for couple of hours each day to tend to his personal needs and care. And to Samantha's delight, Brad's visits continued, and the relationship between them deepened—despite the fact that they had little time alone together.

Brad and Dr. Howard enjoyed animated conversations regarding case histories and options of treatment for various conditions, and Samantha often joined their discussions. Slowly, she and her father became more comfortable with each other.

When her father had been home a little over a week, Samantha noticed that Brad's visits became increasingly more frequent. He was both attentive and affectionate towards her, but he also spent more and more time closeted with her father. Pleased that her father had this distraction from boredom and restlessness, she nevertheless began to feel somewhat left out.

One Saturday, when the two men's discussions had extended well past noon, she interrupted with a sandwich for each of them. They seemed to fall into an uncomfortable silence in her presence, however, so she excused herself. She had turned to leave when her father called her back. "Could you stay for a few minutes, Samantha? We'd like to talk to you." She saw them exchange meaningful glances.

"All right." She walked slowly back into the room, gazing from one to the other.

Brad rose from his chair. "Benton, do you mind if *I* tell Samantha what we've been discussing? Alone?"

"Sure, you do that. But will you stop back in here before you leave?"

Brad nodded, and with his arm loosely around Samantha's shoulders, ushered her from the room. As he guided her towards the main part of the house, she gazed up into his face. "What is it? Is something wrong?"

"Let's find somewhere we can talk without interruption." Brad appeared tense. "How about in here?" He guided her towards the empty sun room, and closed the door.

She turned to face him. "You look so serious. What's going on?"

He indicated the sofa. "Let's sit down."

She perched on the edge, waiting, scrutinizing his expression.

He sat next to her and forearms resting on his knees,

clasped his hands together, studying them for a long moment. Then his gaze rose to meet hers.

"Samantha, your father's asked me to join his medical practice."

She stared at him, and her heart seemed to stop beating.

"As you know, he's going to need help in holding his practice together now, and this is the opportunity of a lifetime for me. Your father's a brilliant man, Samantha. I can learn so much from him." His eyes seemed to plead for understanding.

Samantha struggled to digest the implications of his words. "But what about the group practice? You were looking forward to the diminished demands and stress. I thought that's what you wanted."

"I wanted to want that. For my family's sake and for yours. But the truth is, I could never conjure up much enthusiasm for the job. When your father offered me this partnership, I knew it was what I wanted. Opportunities like this don't come along every day." His dark eyes pinned her with a look of determination, and his tone became one of quiet resolve.

"I've accepted his offer, Samantha."

She stared at him, stunned, the finality of his pronouncement knocking the emotional wind out of her. She rose to her feet. "I see."

Brad remained silent, apparently giving her time to absorb these new developments.

Samantha paced the floor, and gradually, feelings of disillusionment, defeat, and even betrayal seeped in to fill the emptiness that the blow of his words had left. Brad knew how she felt about her father's way of life—that she had little intention of living within its framework—yet he'd made this decision without consulting her, had decided to follow in her father's footsteps. Doing so obviously meant more to him than she did.

She swallowed the lump in her throat and turned to face him. "Congratulations, Brad. If this is what you want, I hope you'll be happy."

He stood and smiled in relief. "It won't change anything between us, Samantha. I promise."

"You're wrong, Brad. It's already changed everything."

"Samantha . . ." She heard the impatience in his tone—so like her father's whenever she complained.

She turned her back on him, walked to the window. "If this is the kind of life you want, then it's just as well we've discovered it now. Before things become any more complicated between us. Because as you know, the lifestyle you're taking on is exactly the kind I want no part of."

He grasped her shoulders and turned her to himself. "I'm not taking on any of his other commitments. We'll have time for us. As far as I'm concerned, our relationship has already progressed too far to turn back."

She shrugged his hands away. "Apparently that's not true. Since you made this decision without consulting me."

He ran a hand through his hair. "I knew you'd object at first. But when you've had a chance to think it over and digest the details, I'm sure you'll agree it's a logical solution. I swear I won't allow it to affect our personal lives to any great extent."

"I've told you, it already has."

His jaw tensed. "Don't do this, Samantha. Give it

time. Let me prove to you that it can work. That we can both have what we want most."

She shook her head. "No. If I continue seeing you, I know I'll be tempted to go along with this charade, and the results would be disastrous. I don't want to live the kind of life my mother did. And I don't want Jonathan to have the kind of childhood I had. If this is your choice, then it's over between us."

"I will control the pace of my own life." He pronounced each word precisely for emphasis. "I've already made my attitude clear to your father."

She shook her head. "You're fooling yourself if you believe that. He'll soon have you doing things his way. Every aspect of his profession is sacred to him. It's an obsession, and he'll never let you turn any part of it into a secondary priority."

"Just the practice, Samantha, I swear. And I'll eventually control my own part of that."

"It will never happen. And I won't be trapped again. I have Jonathan to consider."

His eyes turned hard with determination. "I'll prove to you that you're wrong."

"No, you won't. Because I won't be here to manipulate. Once my father's able to care for himself, Jonathan and I will leave. Our apartment will be ready near the first of the year, and then we'll move on. To lead our own lives."

"I'm in love with you, Samantha. You mean more to me than anything. I'll make you see that."

She laughed at that blatant untruth. "How can you say that with a straight face?" But even now the virile power and masculinity emanating from him threatened to seduce her from her resolve. She raised her chin to resist its effects.

"You can't have it all, Brad." She heard the tremor in her voice and knew she had to get out of there before she crumpled into tears. "You've chosen your life. And it's one that I refuse to share. You knew that before you made your decision." She pulled open the sun room door and fled to her bedroom, her heart breaking.

Brad's first impulse was to go after her, but he held himself in check. He could understand her initial re-action. But she'd come around once she saw that he spoke the truth.

This was, after all, his career they were talking about—the work he would do nearly every day for the rest of his life. Prospects of the group practice left him feeling claustrophobic while the idea of working with Benton Howard filled him with excitement and antic-ipation. Any surgical resident at the hospital would give his eye teeth for an opportunity like this.

He headed back to Benton's bedroom, telling him-self that when Samantha calmed down, she'd listen to reason. He tried to ignore the doubt that had begun to gnaw at the edges of his logic.

By the time he re-entered the bedroom, he couldn't bring himself to return the older man's smile. He walked to the chair he'd vacated earlier and slumped down into it.

"She didn't go for it, huh?"

Brad shook his head, turning to stare out the win-dow at the leaden sky. It suited his mood now.

"Well, you said she might react this way initially. She'll change her mind once she's had time to think things over."

"I hope so. She sounded more adamant than I expected."

"Because you're going into business with me? My own daughter resents me that much?"

"Not you precisely. Your lifestyle."

"My lifestyle? What the heck does that mean?"

"She resents the demands your career has always made on your time. Now I'm becoming your partner."

"That's nonsense. All worthwile careers are demanding. What does she want, some eight-to-five patsy?"

"I think that's exactly what she wants."

"But you said she had no problem with the group practice you were considering?"

"She was moving towards accepting it. We all know that would have been a less demanding alternative."

"But she won't accept your partnership with me. Just how resentful does she feel towards me anyway? Come on, Brad. Level with me."

Brad rose to his feet and paced. "She feels you devoted yourself to your career to the extent that you, Elizabeth, and she had no family life. She wants something better for Jonathan." He saw a flicker of pain in the older man's eyes, and wondered if he'd been unnecessarily blunt. But maybe it was time everyone faced the truth.

"I was earning a living, for cripe's sake! Providing for both Samantha and her mother. She can't seriously doubt that I loved them both more than anything else in this world."

"Have you ever told her that?"

Benton scowled. "I shouldn't have to tell her. She knows I'm not a demonstrative man." His tone turned frustrated. "Who does she think I've worked for all my life?"

"Maybe you should talk to her."

"A man has to have ambition to hold his place in this world. To keep himself and his family financially secure. I learned that lesson very young. She'll realize it too when she's had time to think about it."

"She's been thinking about it for a good part of her life."

"Then she's taken the advantages I provided too much for granted."

Brad paused in his pacing. "I want to make sure you understand exactly where I'm coming from, Benton. We're talking about a long-term arrangement between us. And I'm dead serious when I say that my patients, my practice, and my family—which will eventually include a wife and children—are all that will ever be important to me. With all due respect, as much as I admire you, I don't have your ambition for the other things. I'll probably never author a book, become an adept speaker, or take on the leadership roles you have." He paused to consider his words for a moment. "I think maybe I need people more than you do."

Dr. Howard's eyes narrowed. "I've never heard you talk this way before."

"I've never had to think about it much before."

"Before you began seeing Samantha?"

Brad nodded.

"So you two are seriously considering a future together?"

"*Were* considering, Benton. Past tense. I don't know what's going to happen now."

"Well, well, well." Dr. Howard sunk back onto his pillows and smiled.

When Brad only scowled, he waved a hand in dismissal. "Don't worry about Samantha. She'll come to her senses. And personally, I think you'll change your mind about the limited aspirations after you've been in practice a while. But whether you do or not, you're one of the most talented surgeons I've seen come through here in the past twenty years, and I want you with me." He spread his hands to indicate his position in the bed. "Apart from the fact that I obviously need you right now." He extended a hand towards Brad. "Come over here and let's shake on it."

Brad hesitated. "I mean what I say, Benton. I don't want you to expect more than I can deliver."

"You've laid your position on the line, and I've accepted it. Now come here and shake my hand." Brad reached out tentatively at first, then gripped the older man's hand firmly.

"You still look worried. Believe me, Samantha will come around."

"I sincerely hope so, Benton." But doubt twisted into a knot in the pit of Brad's stomach.

The next week, the hospital buzzed with the news that Brad had accepted a partnership in Benton Howard's practice. And the week after that, his friends gave a party to celebrate the completion of his residency and his good fortune. Samantha attended for appearance's sake, but she stayed only a short while to wish him a perfunctory congratulations.

From that time on, Brad breezed in and out of the Howard home on a regular basis, keeping his senior partner informed of their patients' progress and conferring on options of treatment. He and Samantha treated each other with politeness, but she allowed no familiarity or warmth to redevelop between them, sensing that if she did so, her resolve might falter. Despite the fact that he'd demonstrated how little she meant to him, severing their bond was proving more difficult than she'd anticipated. She began to avoid her father's room and even the house, whenever she knew Brad was there.

But keeping Brad and Jonathan apart became a more difficult task. With Brad at the house so often, the two began spending more and more time together. Often, when Brad had finished his business with her father, he and Jon would go outside to play catch. Late one Saturday morning, Samantha even came upon the two of them watching cartoons in the sun room together, laughing companionably. After that she tried spiriting Jonathan away on errands when she knew Brad was coming, or she tried to distract him with chores or other activities. All of which met with limited success.

And circumstances at school were improving markedly for Jonathan. His friendship with Craig seemed instrumental in getting him included in games and other activities during recess. Now that baseball season had passed, Samantha heard talk of football and even basketball. Jonathan began discussing strategy with his grandfather too and watching football games with him on television.

Then one afternoon, Jonathan came home from school waving a sheet of paper. "Look, Mom! We're having an open house at our school. You'll get to see all the work I've done so far. We're putting all our papers in folders and decorating the classroom."

Samantha perused the printed sheet. The date was

just three days away—at seven in the evening. Attending would pose no problem.

On the appointed day, Josie served them an early dinner, and then Samantha and Jonathan dressed for the open house. Jonathan watched the clock anxiously as Samantha freshened her makeup. "C'mon, Mom, let's go! It's ten minutes to, and it starts at seven."

On the drive over, he strained at his seat belt for a glimpse of the lighted school building, relaxing only slightly when it came into view. "I wish Grampa could've come."

"Maybe next year."

When they entered the classroom, Jonathan ran towards the second desk in the third row. "Wanna see all my stuff?" He shuffled through papers of addition and subtraction problems, proudly displaying his good grades. He showed Samantha his reading worksheets and his art work. He had pulled her over to one wall to admire an exhibit of art projects when his teacher, Mrs. Randolph, joined them.

"Hello, Samantha. Has Jonathan shown you his papers? He's doing excellent work. He's a bright student, like his mother." She turned to Jonathan. "Have you found your art design yet? I put them up this afternoon." They all searched the display for Jonathan's project.

Jon, however, seemed distracted, pausing to glance around the room at frequent intervals. Then suddenly, his voice rang out. "Brad! Over here!"

Samantha whirled around to see Brad making his way towards them. "Hey, Jon," he grinned. "Sorry I'm late."

Samantha glared at him. What was he doing here?

But when his eyes met hers—somehow managing to convey an intimacy—she had to fight to retain her equilibrium. "Hello, Samantha. I hope you don't mind that Jonathan invited me."

"Uh . . . no, of course not." What else could she say with both Jonathan and Mrs. Randolph looking on?

"Why, anyone interested in the children is more than welcome." Mrs. Randolph's bright smile grew thoughtful as she studied Brad. "I know you too, don't I? You were also a student of mine."

Brad grinned. "Yes ma'am, I sure was. Brad Davis."

She grasped the hand he offered her. "Why, of course! Another excellent student." Her gaze returned to Samantha, and her eyes took on an impish gleam. "My, he certainly has grown into a handsome devil, hasn't he? But I'm sure you've noticed that, my dear."

Samantha's face grew hot, and to her chagrin her gaze flew to Brad's.

His eyebrows rose, amused and questioning, and he seemed to await her response.

"Come on, Brad. I'll show you my papers?"

Still smiling, Brad motioned for Samantha to precede him, but she shook her head. "I've already seen them. I'll stay here and look for Jonathan's art work."

Another parent diverted Mrs. Randolph's attention, and she too moved away.

Samantha stood alone, watching Jonathan shuffle through his papers, holding out a few selected ones for Brad's approval. She couldn't take her eyes off Brad. Seeing him unexpectedly like this sharpened a perception that she took great care to suppress these days: Mrs. Randolph was right. He was an extremely attractive man.

Then she observed another student and her mother

at the desk across the aisle from Jonathan's. The woman caught Brad's eye and then spoke to him. The next moment, her eyes glinted with flirtation. Samantha turned away, scanning the exhibited drawings without really seeing them. So most women found him attractive, so what? There was more to a relationship than physical attraction.

Just then she spotted Jonathan's picture. "Oh look, Jonathan! I found it!"

Her son scurried to her side. "Where?"

She smelled Brad's aftershave and knew that he had joined them. She could feel him, standing close behind her. Then his hand touched her waist as he pointed to a picture with Jonathan's name scrawled at the bottom. "Right there, Jon."

She tried to ignore the feelings that his touch aroused, warmth and belonging and a need to feel his arms around her. She stepped away. "And where's that class science project you told me about?"

"Over here." The boy grasped both Samantha and Brad by a hand and pulled them towards a display of various growing plants. As the three of them crossed the room, hand in hand, Samantha's gaze met Brad's over her son's head. His dark eyes held hers, full of meaning, and she had to force herself to look away.

When they'd seen everything, they said their good-byes to Mrs. Randolph. On the way out to the parking lot, Brad announced that he would see them at the Howard home; he needed to talk to Jon's grandfather. "Can I ride with you, Brad?" Jonathan asked. They walked Samantha to her car and then followed her in Brad's SUV.

Arriving at the house, Brad went in to talk to Dr. Howard about the day's patients, and Samantha sent

Jonathan to get ready for bed. After he'd said his good-nights, she tucked him in, then went to the kitchen to fix herself a cup of tea, hoping it would soothe the unsettled emotions the evening had aroused.

Josie had apparently left for the day because only a dim light burned in the empty kitchen. Samantha filled the kettle with water, and when it whistled, poured the steaming liquid into her cup, inhaling the spicy aroma.

Then a movement caught her eye, and she tensed as Brad entered the room. "I'm leaving now."

In putting the hot kettle back on the burner, Samantha noticed her hand tremble and snatched it back, hoping he hadn't noticed. "Good night, Brad. Thank you for coming to Jonathan's open house. I know he appreciated it." She lifted her cup and saucer and attempted to go around him, but he blocked her way.

"Can we talk, Samantha?"

"About what?"

His dark eyes held hers. "I think you can guess."

Her cup rattled in its saucer, and he took it from her and set it on the counter. But he continued to block her path, his bulk emanating a sense of power, which weakened her knees. His scent—part aftershave, part something that was uniquely him—started an awareness building inside her that became more difficult to ignore by the moment. She stepped back. "What is it you want to say, Brad?"

"That tonight felt so right. The three of us. Together. Like a family. I think you felt it too. I know Jonathan did."

She sighed and moved further away. "It's too late for this discussion, Brad. We have no future together any more."

"Don't say that, sweetheart. Give us a chance." He

stepped closer and reached for her; a hand on either side of her waist, he pulled her towards him.

Samantha braced her hands against his upper arms, intending to push him away, but her determination evaporated with the feel of the hard strength beneath her palms. Like a powerless spectator, she watched as he drew her closer. Then as if of their own accord, her hands slid up to curl around his neck.

When his mouth covered hers, the familiar hunger flared. And as his warm lips moved over her own, her head swam, and resistance melted away.

Groaning, Brad broke the kiss and buried his face in the curve of her neck, pressing his lips to the sensitive pulse that pounded there. "I love you, Samantha. I want to marry you." He pulled back to look into her eyes, and his hands slid up to cup her face. "We can work out our problems." His lips were still so close they almost touched hers as he spoke. "I'll make you happy. I swear it."

Samantha went still. *Work out their problems. On his terms.* What was she doing? Letting her attraction to him rule her again.

She twisted free. "I can't start this again, Brad. It's too painful and too hopeless." She turned away because the sight of him weakened her resolve.

But his arms closed around her from behind, and she felt his warm breath as he buried his face in her hair. "We want each other, Sam. We need each other."

"Apparently not enough." She freed herself again and turned to face him. "You had a decision to make, and you made it. But don't try to drag me into the life you've chosen. I've been there, and I won't go back."

Even as she spoke, she remembered the way Jonathan's eyes had brightened when he saw Brad. How he'd grabbed both their hands as he'd pulled them along, joining the three of them together. She closed her eyes. *Jonathan was a child. Too young to know what was good for him.*

"Please Brad," she murmured. "I want you to leave. There's nothing more to say. Except good-night." She turned and fled to her bedroom.

After that night, Samantha tried harder than ever to avoid Brad. She left the house during his visits or stayed out of whatever room he occupied. She also tried again to keep Jonathan away from him but was no more successful than before. Indeed, their friendship seemed to strengthen with each hour they spent together.

And to Samantha's surprise, her father and Jonathan also grew increasingly close as they played board games and watched televised football together. And to her utter amazement, her father seemed to enjoy the camaraderie as much as Jonathan. Once when Samantha had been watching a game with them, Brad came in to discuss a problem, and her father actually asked him to wait until half-time, which was several minutes away.

Then one Saturday after the last football game of the day had ended, Samantha entered the bedroom to find Jonathan curled on the bed beside his grandfather as they perused an old family photograph album.

"Really?" Jonathan exclaimed pointing in fascination at one of the pictures, "that's *your* mom and dad?"

"That's right, son. Your great-grandparents."

Jonathan studied the picture, then peered up into his grandfather's face. "What happened to them?"

Benton Howard's smile faded. "They died, Jonathan." Samantha watched transfixed as a poignant sadness altered her father's features. Rarely had she seen him emotional before—not since her own mother's death, and possibly *never* before that happened.

"When did they die?" Jonathan persisted, but the hush of his tone acknowledged Dr. Howard's somber mood.

"A long time ago. My father died when he was still a relatively young man. Younger than I am now."

A look of alarm crossed Jonathan's face. "You're not going to die, are you Grampa?"

Benton Howard's large arm pulled his grandson into a bear hug of reassurance. "Not for a long, long time, I hope." He, himself, studied the picture for several moments before continuing. "You see, my dad had a lot of problems and a great deal of sadness in his life. I sometimes think he died of a broken heart."

"How come his heart broke?"

Samantha sank into a chair, cringing at Jonathan's persistent questions and expecting an impatient retort from her father. But he continued in a tone of gentle patience. "Well, you see, Jon, my dad never stayed in school as long as his family wanted him to. Never went to college. He became a salesman, though, and a pretty good one while he was a young man. But when he got older, he found it difficult to keep up with the younger men. They began taking over many of his customers. Then finally, he lost his job altogether." Samantha had heard this story only in very abbreviated form and listened in fascination.

"When he couldn't find another job," her father continued, "my parents had trouble paying the taxes on the house we lived in. It belonged to my grandparents, and they lived in it with us. It was a large home in a nice neighborhood, and we all loved it.

"My brother and I were in high school when the troubles began, and we both got part-time jobs to help pay the bills. But we could never earn enough, and we lost Grampa's house." A note of defeat had entered his voice. "My father was very sad and ashamed. He died a short while after that. The doctors said it was a stroke, but . . ." He shrugged and cleared his throat, then turned the album page. "There, see, that's a picture of the house." Samantha sat quietly, almost afraid to breathe, fearing that the slightest distraction might end this precious interlude.

"We went to live with my uncle after that, but his family had a small house and the situation was difficult. My brother and I always felt that we were in the way. One night when we heard our mother crying, my brother and I made a pact that that we'd study hard and go to college. We'd earn enough money to buy our mother another house—one that no one could take away from her or from us again. We even hoped that some day we'd be able to buy back our grandparents' home."

"Did you, Grampa?"

Benton Howard shook his head sadly. "No, Jonathan. The new owners renovated it until it no longer looked like our house, and they refused to sell. Our mother died before we could buy her another one."

He sat in quiet contemplation for several moments. Then his eyes flickered at Samantha, and he cleared his throat again—of emotion or self-consciousness, she wasn't sure. Pulling himself upright, he patted Jonathan's leg and his voice strengthened with forced cheerfulness. "But my brother and I continued to study

and work hard, and we've done pretty well for ourselves. I don't think anyone will ever take our jobs or
our houses away again."

Jonathan's eyes traveled around the room. "This
house, huh Grampa?"

"That's right, son."

Samantha swallowed the lump in her throat. The
story had left her shaken. And given her a new insight
into her father's personality. Why hadn't anyone ever
revealed these details to her before?

Jonathan turned the album page and pointed to another picture. "Are those your parents too?"

Samantha rose from her seat now and walked to the
side of the bed. "I think that's enough for today, Jonathan. Your grandfather's probably getting tired."

Motioning to her that he felt fine, Dr. Howard
chuckled as he observed the picture to which Jonathan
pointed. "No, son. That's your grandmother and I.
When we were young."

"And who's that?"

Benton Howard looked up at his daughter with
amused humor and—could it possibly be?—unconcealed affection. "That's your mother, son. And she's
in that bunny suit because she was in a play when she
was just about your age." Samantha settled onto the
bed on the other side of her son, smiling at the photograph.

Jonathan gazed up at his grandfather. "And did you
and grandma go to watch her in the play?"

Benton's eyes met his daughter's again, but with an
uneasiness this time. "Your grandmother did, but I . . .
had business to attend to."

Samantha felt the familiar bristle of resentment for
just a moment, but in view of the revelations of the

past few minutes, a pang of regret and sadness replaced her hostile feelings.

Jonathan turned the page and pointed to another picture. "Is that you too, Mom?"

"Yup, that's me. All dressed up for my junior prom."

Her father pointed to her escort in the picture. "And who's this fellow? I don't think I like his looks."

"That's Gordon Baker, Dad. You never met him, but you're right, you wouldn't have liked him. He was arrogant and irresponsible. But good-looking enough to attract the girls anyway." She looked up to smile teasingly at her father, but he had turned somber and stared at the page.

Jonathan pointed to yet another picture. "How come you're wearing that funny hat in this one, Mom?"

Samantha laughed. "That's my high school graduation picture. People wear caps and gowns like that when they graduate."

Still unsmiling, Benton Howard spoke softly. "At least I made it for part of that one, huh?" He paused and their eyes met again. "I stayed until you'd gone up to the podium to receive your diploma before leaving." Samantha nodded and then tensed in bewilderment as Benton Howard reached over to include her in the circle of his arm. "I missed a few things, didn't I?" Then to her utter amazement he pulled her closer and placed a light kiss on her forehead. "I'm sorry, baby," he whispered.

Afterwards, Samantha couldn't stop thinking about her father's revelations and his mellowed attitude. She'd actually sensed a vulnerability in him as he'd told Jonathan about his family's financial problems.

Before today, *vulnerable* would have been the last word she'd have used to describe her father.

Also his disclosures had left her feeling guilty for never having tried to understand the reasons behind his addiction to his work. Had her mother known? She must have.

Samantha could remember one or two occasions on which her parents had referred to the fact that the Howard family had been poor—that her father'd had to struggle for everything he'd attained. But they had never gone into any detail, and Samantha had never asked. Now she wondered why.

Chapter Seven

T hat night, after tucking Jonathan into bed, Samantha sank down into the living room sofa to read the newspaper. As she sat chuckling over a comic strip, the doorbell rang. Checking her watch, she noted that it was nine-thirty. Who would be calling at this hour on a Sunday night? Opening the door, she found herself staring up at Brad, huddled deep in an overcoat. A cold, biting wind accompanied him into the house before she could push the door closed again.

"I'm sorry to come so late, but I had an emergency at the hospital and wanted your father to see some of the lab reports. On top of that, I had car trouble on the way over. Is Benton still awake?"

"I'm sure he is. I heard his television a few minutes ago." She offered to take Brad's coat.

"Don't bother to hang it. I'll only stay a few minutes." He shrugged out of it.

When she took it from him, the cold permeating the

garment made her shiver. "Brrr . . . it's nippy out there. We must be in for an early winter."

"A few snow flurries fell on my way over," he told her as she laid the coat over a chair. These few polite words constituted the most pleasant exchange they'd had since the night of Jonathan's open house.

Brad lingered. "Don Edwards told me he wants your father to start getting out of bed and into a chair in a day or so."

"That's good, isn't it?" Realizing that she hadn't sounded elated, Samantha gave a weak laugh and hurried to explain. "I'm happy that Dad's progressing so well, of course, but his enforced leisure seems to have brought out the best in him. He's so much more relaxed and communicative than ever before. He and Jonathan are becoming close. I guess I hate to see the inevitable end of it all when Dad's up and around again."

"It'll be quite some time before he's able to return to work. You'll have him around for a while."

His gaze lingered on her a moment before he excused himself and headed for Dr. Howard's room.

Samantha stood in the foyer looking after him. It felt nice to have a civil conversation again. She realized—as she had once before—that she'd confided in him because he seemed to really care. Perhaps there was no harm in talking, as long as she didn't allow sentiment to overcome logic.

Samantha returned to the living room sofa and retrieved the newspaper. She had almost finished a front-page article when the doorbell rang again.

This time when Samantha opened the door, she was surprised to see the nurse who had flirted with Brad at Carol's party. "Can you tell me how much longer

Brad will be detained? He said just a few minutes, and I'm getting cold out in the car."

Samantha stared mutely before collecting herself enough to invite the woman in.

Brad had either heard the doorbell or finished his business, because he returned to the foyer just then. "I'm sorry, Adrian. That took a little longer than I expected." He gave her an apologetic grimace. Then gazing from her to Samantha, he added. "You two know each other, right?"

"Yes, of course." Adrian's forced smile contained little warmth.

Brad retrieved his coat from the chair and shrugged into it. "The tow truck's on its way. We'd better get back to my car." They bade Samantha a hasty good-bye and departed.

As she closed the door behind them, a sick knot tightened in the pit of her stomach. So, Brad had begun seeing other women.

She stole into the darkened dining room and through the sheer curtains watched as he helped Adrian into her car, then hurried to the passenger side. A moment later, they sped off.

Well, Samantha thought, he'd obviously gotten over their own failed relationship. She supposed it was inevitable that he would start dating again; she just hadn't expected it so soon. Nor had she expected it to hurt so much. But Brad was an attractive man, headed for a distinguishing career. Women would pursue him more than ever.

She made her way back to the living room and dropped onto the sofa. Maybe it was time she got on with her own life as well. Her friend Becky, a nurse at the hospital, had been trying for some time to arrange a blind date between Samantha and her brother. Samantha had resisted until now, but perhaps she should reconsider. She'd talk to Becky tomorrow. Samantha chalked up her lack of enthusiasm to end-of-the-day fatigue and headed off to bed.

They went out the following Saturday evening, a double date with Becky and her fiancee. Ben was attractive, polite, and refined, and the four of them had a pleasant evening. Why then, Samantha asked herself after he had taken her home, could she summon no enthusiasm for the follow-up date they'd planned for next weekend?

Over the course of the next several days, the necessity of watching Brad come and go on his visits to her father did nothing to increase Samantha's eagerness for her upcoming date. Perhaps her father's eventual return to work would have one advantage she hadn't foreseen. Without Brad around as a constant reminder of what might have been, she could develop some interest in a life that did not include him.

Towards the end of that week, Benton Howard got out of bed and into a chair for the first time since the accident. His doctor advised him to do so twice a day thereafter in order to begin regaining his strength.

Walking back from the cafeteria, after lunch the following day, Samantha described to Maggie the characteristic determination with which her father had hauled himself out of bed and into his chair. Then while waiting for Maggie to unlock the office door, she spied Brad coming down the corridor towards them. Samantha braced herself for the tumultuous feelings he always evoked.

Brad greeted Maggie, who then rushed into the office to answer a ringing telephone, then turned to Samantha. "I hear your father got into a chair with no problems yesterday."

"Yes, I was just telling Maggie about it. I had trouble convincing him to get back into bed."

"His doctor tells me he'd like to get him into a wheelchair for extended periods before long. Maybe crutches in a couple of weeks." He grinned, inviting a like response from her, and she obliged.

"Would you believe that Dad and Jonathan are already planning the snowman they'll build together with the first snowfall?" She laughed and the sound of gaiety in her tone surprised her. Why did she—even now—find it so hard to control her response to this man? Why did she so easily find herself caught up in his moods and ensnared by his magnetism?

Brad's grin widened. "So, the family bonding continues?"

Samantha nodded. "I just hope Dad doesn't drop Jonathan too abruptly when he's up and around again. Jon's become very fond of him, depends on his company now."

"Only Jonathan?"

She gave a reluctant smile. "I guess I've enjoyed this new, warmer side of him too. But I know what to expect when things get back to normal. Jonathan doesn't."

Brad reached out to cup Samantha's chin with his hand. "Try not to be too cynical. Your father sounds like he's enjoying himself too."

She fought the usual response to his touch and stepped back, reminding herself that he'd been with Adrian just last week and possibly since then.

Then someone called her name, and Samantha turned to see Becky coming towards them. "Tom and I have tickets for the same play that you and Ben are seeing tomorrow night," she told Samantha. "How about the four of us meeting for a quick bite beforehand? After that, we promise we'll leave you two alone for the rest of the evening."

"Uh, sure. That'll be fine."

"Good." Becky sniggered. "I'll tell Ben it was your idea so he won't be angry with me. I'm sure he'd rather have you all to himself." With a wave she hurried off.

When Samantha turned back to Brad, her gaze collided with his angry one. "Who in the devil is Ben?"

"Becky's brother. I went out with him for the first time last week. We have another date for tomorrow night."

Brad's jaw tensed. "Cancel it," he growled.

"I certainly won't." She raised her chin. "Besides, you're dating again. Why should you object if I do?"

His brow furrowed. "Me? Who am I dating?"

"Adrian."

"For cripe's sake, Samantha. She just happened to drive by the night my car broke down and offered me a ride."

"I saw the way she looks at you."

A slow smile crept across Brad's face. "Do I detect a note of jealousy?"

Samantha gave a dismissive laugh. "Dream on, Brad."

"Okay, I will. I think you went out with what's-her-name's brother in retaliation. Because you thought I was seeing Adrian."

She crossed her arms in front of her. "You've got quite an ego, you know that?"

"Now that you know the truth, you can call off your date."

Indignation flared at his arrogance—before the sad reality of their situation snuffed it out. She sighed. "How many times do we have to go over this, Brad? There's no hope for us. We can't agree on the most basic tenets of living. The biggest favor we can do ourselves is to forget one another and move on."

Brad's jaw set in determination. "Have you seen me do anything other than tend to your father's practice? When he comes back to work, my responsibilities will lessen even further. Time will prove to you that things can work between us."

"When my father returns to work, he'll prove just the opposite to both of us. He'll be off and running again and take you with him." She shook her head. "The time line for slowing down is always just around the corner for you, isn't it? Problem is, we never quite get there before new demands pop up."

"When your father's back on his feet, he and I will begin a long-term arrangement that we've both agreed to. You'll see that my responsibilities will lessen. Then you and I can start making our own plans." His gaze hardened. "Until then, I don't want you to date other men, Samantha."

"You have nothing to say about it."

"Don't I?" A determined gleam flashed in his eyes, and gripping her upper arm, he propelled her across the corridor into an empty conference room.

As he shut them inside, Samantha pulled free of his grasp. "What do you think you're doing?" She turned to pull the door open again, but Brad's hand slammed against it. When she turned to face him in indignation, his other hand slammed to the other side of her, boxing her in.

She pressed her back to the door as he moved in close. "I could call this sexual harassment and cause you a lot of trouble."

"I don't think you will." Stepping even closer, he spoke her name in a low, seductive tone. "When you're out with your boyfriend tomorrow night, I want you to remember what it's like when we're together." His voice dropped to a whisper. "There's a chemistry between us, Samantha. You can't deny that."

She forced herself to look him in the eye. "No, I can't. But a serious commitment involves more than chemistry." Her rational argument belied the jelly-like quality permeating her legs as his lips descended to within an inch of her own.

Then as his masculine scent surrounded her, she felt her resistance slip further. When he pressed his face into her hair and murmured her name again, it took every ounce of her will to keep from reaching for him.

He nuzzled her neck, and his coaxing lips and warm breath sent a shudder of anticipation through her. Then once again, his mouth moved to within an inch of her own. "We belong together, Samantha," he whispered hoarsely. "You know we do." When his mouth covered hers, she whimpered and melted against him. His arms closed around her, and she slid her own arms inside his jacket and around his waist. His body shuddered with the contact, and he deepened their kiss with a low groan.

Then suddenly voices sounded outside the door. Somebody turned the knob, and shook it against its locked resistance. A masculine voice grumbled something about a key.

Brad ignored them, and his hands came up to cup her face. "I love you, Samantha. I can't stand the thought of you with someone else. Please don't give up on us. We can work out our problems."

She stared up into his face, wanting his lips to cover hers again but struggling to concentrate on his words. "Work them out how?"

"With common sense and compromise, sweetheart."

Reality seeped back into her emotion-fogged mind. "While you remain in my father's practice?"

Anxiety flickered in his eyes. "We can do it, I promise you."

She pulled herself from his embrace and shook her head. "What are we doing? Nothing has changed." When he tried to take her into his arms again, she backed away.

"Nothing *has* to change, Samantha," he persisted. "We'll work out the present circumstances to both our satisfaction."

"You keep saying that! And I keep telling you that's not possible." Her gaze hardened. "You aren't the kind of man I want, Brad. I'm sorry, but you don't even come close." She drew a deep breath and wrapped her arms around her middle. "I can't let myself be ruled by physical attraction—for Jonathan's sake as well as my own. If you really care about us then please, let us look for lasting happiness. Elsewhere."

"Where, with him? With what's-her-name's brother?" He took a step towards her, and she pointed a determined finger at him. "Don't Brad, it's over between us. I'm going to move on. I suggest you do the same." She pulled open the door and escaped down the hallway.

Brad remained in the conference room after she'd gone, overcome with feelings of frustration and defeat. Why couldn't he get through to her?

A sinking feeling filled him. Or had he been kidding himself all along? Maybe Samantha would never make a doctor's wife. Her words came back to him: *We can't agree on the most basic tenets of living. If you really care about us, let us look for lasting happiness elsewhere.* Was it possible this other man really interested her?

And did she truly need more time and attention than he, himself, could ever give her? He'd refused to consider that possibility, but maybe the time had come to face reality.

A reality about which he could do nothing.

He'd chosen his profession long ago, had prepared for it almost since adolescence. It was too late to change direction. Medicine was a part of him now. No other field even remotely interested him.

And now that he thought about it—given the strength of Samantha's convictions—even the demands of the group practice would probably have been too much for her. But that possibility was out of the question now, because to him the difference between the group and Benton's practice was like serfdom versus unlimited potential.

A feeling of desolation washed over him. Samantha was right. They wanted and needed different things. And their diverse needs precluded a future together. It was time he stopped deluding himself. Samantha had to go her way, and he had to go his.

He straightened and expelled a shaky breath. So that was it, then. It was over. He closed his eyes against the pain.

It would all become easier, when Benton was on his feet, and he didn't have to keep going to that house. Without the constant contact, maybe he could begin building a life without her.

Brad left the room and closed the door behind himself. He started down the hospital corridor, unable to shake the feeling that he was beginning a new and very lonely journey.

Chapter Eight

Brad pulled to the curb behind the red sports car. He couldn't believe he was doing this.

That nurse at the hospital yesterday—Becky—had said she'd see Samantha for dinner around seven tonight. Which meant her brother would probably pick Samantha up shortly before that. Brad checked his watch: six-twenty and the guy was already here. Eager little twerp.

Brad wasn't sure why he should care. He really had accepted the fact that he and Samantha were past history. But for some reason, he had to get a look at the guy she'd chosen to replace him. He climbed from his car and had gotten about halfway to the door when it opened.

Samantha stepped outside, followed by a sandy-haired young man of medium height. They were laughing as they came out onto the front porch, but Samantha's smile faded when she saw Brad.

Taking a deep breath, he continued towards them.

As they neared one another, Samantha's gaze met his, and she uttered a subdued hello. Then pausing, she introduced the two men, explaining to Ben that Brad was her father's business partner. The two shook hands and exchanged a few polite words.

Watching them, Samantha's own reaction discomforted her. She had thought of Ben as reasonably good-looking, but next to Brad he appeared slight and colorless. And while Brad exuded an aura of sensual masculinity, Ben appeared almost prim.

Angry, she chastised herself. Ben was decent and polite and being with him was quietly pleasant. Much the opposite of Brad, who always managed to jumble her emotions.

Besides, Brad belonged to her past now. She really did intend to move on. She enjoyed Ben's company, and for now, that was enough.

After a short and courteous exchange, Samantha and Ben continued towards his car. When he'd closed her inside, and she fumbled with her seat belt, she could see out of the corner of her eye that Brad still stood on the front porch. She continued to stare straight ahead, however, as Ben started the car and pulled away from the house.

And as the evening wore on, to Samantha's dismay, thoughts of Brad kept intruding on her consciousness. She had to force herself to join in the general conversation at dinner and then to concentrate on the performance of the play.

When the evening had drawn to a close, and Ben left her on her doorstep with only a light kiss on the cheek, Samantha realized that she liked him very much and that a friendship was developing between them.

But only that: friendship. Their relationship contained no physical attraction—for either of them, apparently.

However, they enjoyed spending time together and felt comfortable in each other's company. Indeed, they had discovered a mutual interest in downhill skiing. Ben had invited Samantha to join himself, Becky, and a group of friends on a New Year's weekend ski trip at a northern Michigan resort.

Thanksgiving drew near, and on a Sunday afternoon when Jonathan was out playing, Samantha entered her father's room to discuss the holiday dinner menu, unsure of what degree of enthusiasm to expect from him.

To her surprise and pleasure, he took an active interest in planning the menu and particularly requested her mother's special sweet potato casserole. Then a gleam of excitement appeared in his eyes. "What would you think of inviting your Uncle Mark and his family for Thanksgiving dinner? I haven't seen my brother in over a year."

When Samantha assented, he eagerly suggested that they substitute the planned apple pie with his own mother's chocolate pecan pie and surprise Uncle Mark. He went on to tell Samantha what an excellent cook his mother had been.

"You've never spoken much about your parents or your childhood until recently."

His memory-glazed eyes came to focus on her. "I know, honey. I suppose that's because so many of the memories are painful ones."

"I never knew the details of your family's financial problems until you talked to Jonathan about them." She twisted the sapphire ring on her right hand, trying to disguise the hurt she felt.

His eyes softened. "Telling Jonathan was my way of telling you too, Samantha. Brad mentioned that you'd felt neglected as a child because of the hours I spent away from home. I'd never thought much before about how all-consuming I'd allowed my work to become over the years. Once I began to analyze it, I realized I wanted you to understand something of my motivation. I'm selfish enough to want my daughter to see me as someone other than a cold and self-serving man."

"Oh, Dad . . ." She wanted to say so much, but her brain went numb, and she felt tongue-tied. True they'd talked more in recent weeks, but this kind of intimate sharing was something new between them.

Her father lay his head against the back of his chair. "Brad said something else that gave me food for thought . . . and thought is something I've had plenty of time for these past weeks." He rolled his eyes. "He made it clear that he intends to limit his career to our practice and our patients. That he didn't have my interest in the other endeavors. He said he needs people more than I do and that he always intends to make as much time as possible for family—present and future.

"That young man made me realize that deep down, I need people too, and maybe I'd better start letting the ones that matter know so." He gave her a lingering and meaningful look.

Samantha swallowed against a cacophony of emotions. "Jonathan and I need you too, Dad. And sorry as we are about your accident, we've loved having you at home."

They'd been sitting in adjoining chairs, separated by a small table, and now Benton Howard reached across and squeezed his daughter's hand. "I intend to continue spending more time with the two of you. Even after I go back to work."

Her eyes misted. "I'm so glad."

An uncomfortable silence followed, and Samantha surmised that her father was as overcome as she was with this newfound sharing. But her heart pounded on yet another account. "When did you and Brad discuss all of this?"

"Before he'd officially accepted my offer to join the practice. He wanted me to know where he stood before we made a formal commitment, refused to come in with me unless I agreed. And believe me, he meant business."

"And you *did* agree?"

"You bet. It was either that or lose him. And the more we work together, the more I see that he meant what he said. I tried to get him to take on a couple of speaking engagements, and he adamantly refused. Got hot under the collar when I pressed."

A sick lump rose in Samantha's throat. What had she done?

"Yes sir, Brad got me thinking," Dr. Howard continued. "I've forgotten what family fun is, by gosh, and if I'm going to experience any during my lifetime, I'd better get started. I'm not a young man anymore."

Samantha opened her mouth to deny the implication that he was getting old, but he hurried on. "And you know what else? That six-year-old grandson of mine is helping me to relearn what fun can be." His smile made him look younger than he had in years.

"Do you suppose that this accident was a blessing in disguise?" He chuckled. "Disguised in a lot of pain and inconvenience?" But then his gaze turned thoughtful. "Maybe the man upstairs is giving me a chance to see what I've missed all these years." He held up a finger to make his point. "That's not to say I don't enjoy my work, but maybe it's time for a little balance. I'm thinking of giving up some of my duties unrelated to my practice."

Samantha stared at him. "Are you serious?"

"I haven't made any definite decisions about what to eliminate yet, but it's time some of the younger men took over." He grinned, and when a mischievous sparkle appeared in his eyes, Samantha wondered if she were catching a glimpse of the young and carefree man he'd once been. "There is one *new* responsibility I've been thinking of undertaking, however."

Her smile faltered. "What's that?"

"Little League coach for my grandson's baseball team!"

Without thinking, Samantha jumped up to plant a kiss on his cheek. "Daddy, Jonathan will love that!" Then realizing how uncharacteristic of their relationship such an overt display of affection was, her face grew hot.

But her father snatched her hand and gave it another squeeze. "We'll both enjoy it." He chuckled again. "Maybe Brad would like to be my assistant. No reason we wouldn't work well together as coaches too."

His gaze became thoughtful, and he gave her another meaningful look. "If my practice weren't in Brad's hands, my recuperation would be a much more nervewracking ordeal. He's a fine young man and a fine doctor. I don't know anyone who doesn't like and respect Brad."

Only she had misjudged him and insulted his integrity, Samantha thought. Or had she?

Brad had, after all, made the all-important decision

to join her father's practice without consulting her—a decision that would affect both their lives as well as Jonathan's if they pursued a future together. Didn't that imply that his career took precedence over their relationship?

Or were her continued doubts immature and self-centered? Samantha's mind reeled with the afternoon's revelations and the questions they'd evoked.

Her father seemed to sense this and veered to a more neutral topic. "So, what do you think of my Thanksgiving idea? Shall we invite Uncle Mark? It would sure be great to see him again."

"I think it's a wonderful idea. Would you like to call him or shall I?"

Dr. Howard reached for the telephone. "I'll do it. And right now."

Samantha got up to leave but paused at the door.

"Dad?" He looked up. "Why . . . I mean . . . it seems strange that I've never heard the details of your family's problems before. That even Mother never told me."

Dr. Howard set the telephone down. "We were married a long time before I told your mother all the details. Maybe, knowing how painful the telling was for me, she never repeated it." He paused for several moments. "I guess it always seemed that revealing the story was somehow a betrayal of my father. He endured such shame and humiliation, thinking that he'd let us all down. Also I never wanted you to think of your grandfather as a failure." His eyes came up to look intently into her own. "Because he wasn't a failure as a human being. He was a warm, caring, and responsible man. And that's why I think that his shame might be part of what killed him."

Samantha gave him a nod of understanding. "Thank you for telling me now, Dad." She smiled. "Say hello to Uncle Mark for me."

Her uncle and his family accepted their invitation with pleasure. And Dr. Howard worked the entire week before the holiday on maneuvering himself into a wheelchair so that he could spend the day in the living room and join the family at the dinner table.

Although the weather earlier in the week had been cold and rainy with some wet snow, Thanksgiving Day itself dawned clear, sunny, and brisk. Samantha hurried around in the morning and early afternoon, adding last-minute touches to the food and the table. Josie had done much of the preliminary work earlier in the week and had also left the house in spotless order.

When the time for their guests' arrival drew near, Jonathan sat in the front window, watching for their car. "Here comes one, and it's slowing down!" he announced excitedly. And then even more excitedly, he jumped to his feet. "Hey, it's Brad!" Samantha's breath caught until Jon added a note of disappointment. "Oh. He's going next door." After a few moments, his voice rang out again. "Trevor just ran out of the house to meet him. I didn't know Trevor was here! Can I go see him, Mom?"

Knowing they would have no children for Jonathan to play with at their own gathering, Samantha agreed. "But don't stay too long. And if they sit down to dinner, you come home."

"Okay, Mom, I promise." He ran to his room for his jacket, then raced out the door.

Wiping sticky hands on a kitchen towel, Samantha

moved to a front window to watch Jonathan hurry towards the Davis house, calling out and waving. Trevor ran to greet him, and Brad stopped to wait for the boys before going inside, pausing to ruffle Jonathan's hair as he joined them. Samantha stepped behind the curtain as Brad glanced towards the Howard house.

Twenty minutes later, their own guests arrived from the Detroit area. Samantha's father and his brother greeted each other with handshakes, bear hugs, and much back slapping, while Samantha embraced her Aunt Katherine. Uncle Mark produced two bottles of champagne, and with smiles and loud toasts, they hailed their reunion.

The two families exchanged news on the latest developments in their lives. Mark and Katherine's son was away at law school on the west coast and would be returning home for the Christmas holidays.

As they talked, Samantha's eye kept roving to the window, through which she could clearly see the Davis house. Jonathan and Trevor had come out into the front yard to play football and had been kicking and throwing the ball around for a few minutes when Brad joined them. Samantha watched as he took the ball from Trevor and motioned for the boys to move back several feet. He then alternated throwing passes to first one and then the other. He stood with his back towards the Howard house, wearing snug jeans and a short windbreaker jacket, the combination of which accentuated his narrow hips and broad shoulders. The sight of him aroused a stir of awareness, which Samantha quashed with a sigh of irritation.

Turning back to the conversation, she noticed that her aunt's gaze had followed her own to the scene outside. "Looks like the neighbors have dinner guests too. Are the little ones their grandchildren?"

"The boy in the blue jacket is their grandson, but the one in the red," Samantha couldn't help smiling with pride, "is my son, Jonathan."

Benton Howard adjusted the wheels of his chair so that he too could peer out the window. "And that's Brad, the young man who joined my practice. I told you about him, Mark." He turned to Samantha. "Call Brad over, Sam. I want Mark to meet him." To his brother, he added, "And wait until you meet my grandson. He's quite a boy!"

Samantha pulled herself from her chair. She'd hardly spoken to Brad since that day, over two weeks ago, when he'd arrived just as she and Ben were leaving on their date. Lately he'd taken to calling her father on the telephone rather than stopping at the house to discuss their patients. The last few times he *had* stopped by, he'd done so while Samantha was at work.

She'd decided to try and talk to him about the revelations her father had made but hadn't summoned the courage. Brad seemed so determined to avoid her. At the hospital, they spoke only as much as common courtesy demanded. Their last argument—and final breakup—seemed to stand like a barrier between them, and now as Samantha moved towards the front door, her heart pounded.

"Brad?" she called out, and his head came up with a jerk. "Would you come over here for a few minutes, please? Dad would like you to meet his brother."

He hesitated for a moment, and then after a few words to the boys, they all headed for the house.

Samantha stepped aside as they entered, greeting Trevor first and then Brad, who uttered a perfunctory

"Happy Thanksgiving" without a hint of the familiar smile.

"Come in here!" Dr. Howard's voice rang out. "I want all of you to meet my brother!"

Jonathan went to stand by the wheelchair, and his grandfather pulled him close in an affectionate hug, introducing him to their guests with unconcealed pride. Then he proceeded to introduce Trevor and finally, Brad.

They all shook hands and progressed to a lively conversation, except for Samantha, who remained self-consciously quiet. Then Uncle Mark asked her if she had another glass so that Brad could join them in a flute of champagne. When she handed it to him, Brad barely glanced her way. His thank you sounded perfunctory and cool.

"My brother's told me a lot about you," Uncle Mark informed Brad.

"All good, Brad. All good," Dr. Howard assured. "I had to do some fast talking to get this boy to join my practice on such short notice," he continued. "He already had something else lined up, and needed to make a quick decision. And believe me, it was a tough . . . one for him." Benton's words faltered, and his gaze flew to Samantha, then to Brad, obviously realizing that he'd introduced a touchy subject. He coughed and turned his attention to his grandson, giving him another hug. "And this guy's my football buddy. Tell Uncle Mark about the game we watched last Saturday, Jon."

Samantha gazed down into her lap, twirling the ring on her right hand. If it had been such a difficult decision for Brad, why hadn't he asked her to help him make it? And if she had been aware of all the facts back then, would it have made a difference to her? She wasn't sure.

She looked up to find Brad watching her with emotionless eyes. Then after a moment, he averted them. After that he seemed to ignore her again, even when her father addressed her in an effort to include her in the conversation.

And once when they'd all been talking and laughing, and she ventured to inject a comment, Brad's smile faltered as his gaze met hers. Then immediately, he'd looked away.

Soon afterward, the telephone rang. Mrs. Davis had dinner ready next door and asked Samantha to send Brad and Trevor home. Then she paused. "Oh Samantha, you're not spending the holiday alone, are you? Because the three of you are certainly welcome to join us. I don't know why I didn't think of it sooner."

Samantha thanked her and explained about their guests.

When she delivered Mary's message, Brad bid the others good-bye but his gaze continued to avoid Samantha. Then after exchanging a few words with Dr. Howard about a patient with whom they were having problems, Brad and Trevor headed for the door. Samantha followed to see them out.

Outside, Trevor ran toward the Davis house, and Brad started to follow, then stopped. He turned to Samantha, the guarded look still in his eyes. "You know, for what it's worth, I was wrong for not consulting you before deciding to join your father's practice." Then his mouth twisted in a humorless smile. "But as it turned out, that was a minor detail, wasn't it? What with everything else we had going against us."

Samantha searched his eyes, trying to ascertain

whether this was an overture or a rebuke. But before she could speak, he turned and hurried away.

She tried to forget him and enjoy the holiday, but to her own annoyance, she couldn't regain her festive spirit.

"Is your neighbor, Brad, married?" Samantha jumped at her aunt's question as they all sat around the dinner table.

"No. No, he isn't."

"My, he's so handsome. In my day, young women wouldn't let a catch like him run around single for long."

Samantha gave her aunt a *go figure* shrug, but felt the stiffness of her own smile. Then catching her father's eye, she flushed under his knowing gaze.

Thereafter, despite her own subdued feelings, Samantha tried to present a cheerful facade for the sake of the others. Her father and Uncle Mark hadn't seen each other in a long time, and she didn't want to dampen the gaiety of the occasion.

Late that evening, as they saw their guests to the door, Samantha couldn't help glancing towards the spot where Brad had parked his car. Why was the fact that it was still there a source of comfort to her?

Late the following morning, Cindy and Trevor appeared at the back door. While the boys ran off to play, Cindy and Samantha enjoyed a cup of tea and a rare opportunity to chat. After they'd exchanged news of the major happenings in their lives, Cindy gave Samantha a thoughtful look. "My mother said you and Brad were seeing each other for a while this fall."

Samantha shifted uncomfortably. "Uh, yes. Sort of."

"But you're not any more?"

Samantha shook her head.

"What happened, Sam?"

Samantha shrugged. "It's complicated. Partly misunderstandings."

"Can't you guys talk over the misunderstandings?"

"He's not very talkative these days."

"Do you want me to speak to him? I could . . ."

"No! This is between Brad and me. We'll discuss it someday."

"Someday? I swear, Sam . . ." But when she saw the look on her friend's face, Cindy held up her hands in surrender. "Okay. All right. It's none of my business. But we were hoping you guys would get together."

She took a sip of her tea and gave Samantha a sidelong glance. "Is whatever happened between the two of you the reason Brad's been so down lately?"

"I didn't realize he was."

"My parents say he's been absolutely morose for the past few weeks, and Bob and I definitely noticed it yesterday. He didn't crack a smile all day, and he hardly said two words during dinner. Even Trevor noticed."

She paused. "Is everything all right between your father and Brad?"

"Couldn't be better."

Cindy sighed and shrugged. "Oh, well. Brad's a big boy. I guess he can take care of himself."

Chapter Nine

Now that Thanksgiving was over, the family at the Howard house began making plans for the Christmas season. Jonathan wanted a large tree and pleaded to get it as soon as possible. They decided that if they cut a fresh one, even if they decorated it early, it would likely stay soft through the holiday season. They planned to cut it the first weekend in December.

Dr. Howard was getting around on crutches now and eager to get out of the house. He suggested that if they didn't take too long in selecting the tree, he could go along for the ride and enjoy the fun from the car. He still wasn't adept enough on crutches to maneuver over uneven ground.

At ten o'clock the following Sunday morning, they helped Grandpa into the front passenger seat of Samantha's compact car, and set out. Frost still lay on the ground and the air crackled with the cold, but the sun shone brightly in a clear blue sky.

Arriving at the tree farm, they parked in a spot that would afford Dr. Howard the best view of a promising-looking grove. Trying to stay as much as possible within his sight, Samantha and Jonathan set out on their search for the perfect Christmas tree. They found it within a relatively short time, and although Grandpa could see only about half of it from his seat in the car, he signaled his approval.

Jonathan and Samantha took turns sawing at the trunk, and when the tree finally fell, the proprietor of the farm helped them secure it to the top of the car. As they tied it into place, Samantha realized that it was a good deal larger than it had appeared out in the field. On the drive home, she began to worry whether she had the strength to get it down and drag it into the house by herself. She could, of course, expect little help from Jonathan and none from her father.

Then as they neared the house, Samantha recognized the vehicle parked in the driveway. Help was waiting for them. They pulled in behind the green SUV and saw Brad descend the porch steps and come towards them. When the car stopped, Jonathan jumped out. "See our Christmas tree, Brad! Isn't it a big one?"

"It sure is." Brad's gaze scanned the length of the tree, and he turned to Samantha. "How did you plan to get that thing into the house by yourself?" His tone held a mixture of amusement and irritation.

Samantha laughed. "I have to admit I've been a little worried about that. It didn't look that big when we were cutting it."

"Will you help us, Brad?" Jonathan's eyes shone with delight.

"I guess I'd better." He looked up at the now leaden sky and the snowflakes that had begun to fall. "But first let's get your grandfather inside. The sidewalks will be slippery soon."

"Okay." Jonathan stuck out his tongue to catch a falling flake and then ran to hold the door open as Brad helped the older man into the house.

Once they'd settled Dr. Howard in his wheelchair, the three younger people worked together to get the tree into the house. Jonathan persuaded them to take it right into the living room so they could begin decorating it soon. Samantha retrieved the tree stand from the garage, and Brad helped them lower the tree into it while Samantha tightened the screws that held it upright.

"Can we start decorating it, Mom?"

Samantha fell into a nearby chair. "Oooh Jonathan, maybe we'd better leave that for another day. I'm pooped."

"But Brad might not be here to help us another day."

"I can't stay today, Jon. I just stopped by to discuss a few things with your grandfather, and then I have to get back to the hospital."

"Will you come back tomorrow?"

Brad's gaze flickered at Samantha. "Uh . . . I don't think so, Jon."

"Brad's very busy with Grandpa's practice. I think we can manage to decorate the tree by ourselves." But she smiled hesitantly at Brad. "Of course, Brad's welcome to join us if he gets some free time."

He avoided her gaze. "We'll see."

Then he addressed his partner. "I'd like to talk to you about Harold Wilson, the colostomy I did on Tuesday. He's having problems."

Dr. Howard nodded. "Let's go into the library."

When they'd left, Jonathan cajoled Samantha into returning to the garage with him to find the tree ornaments. Together they pulled two large cartons from a cupboard and opened them. Jonathan oooh'd and aaah'd over the contents. Then, laden with armloads of small boxes, they returned to the living room.

Carefully removing some of the more delicate decorations, Samantha began setting them on one of the tables. She handled each one tenderly, savoring its familiarity and the childhood memories it recalled. She started to tell the story behind one of them to Jonathan, but discovered that he'd gone back to the garage for more.

Finally, Samantha unpacked the tree-top angel, glittering all white and silver and gold. She gazed at it with special fondness, deciding that its deteriorated condition only added to its charm. They'd had it since she was a small child, and it had always been a special favorite.

As she examined it, handling it gingerly, she sensed someone at her elbow and turned to find Brad also gazing down at it. The poignancy of his smile held her spellbound, and she realized how long it had been since she'd last seen him smile.

He took the angel from her, brushing her fingers with his own as he did so. "I remember this. You've had it since we were kids. Poor thing's close to disintegrating, isn't it?"

Her fingertips still tingled with his touch, and Samantha turned to the boxes on the floor to conceal her feelings, pulling out a painted, wooden snowman. "We've had a lot of these since I was a child."

Brad pointed to a faded red bauble, depicting a barely discernible nativity scene. "My parents have one like this one." Then he picked up a crudely-made bird ornament and grinned. "You made this one in grade school, remember? It's supposed to be a dove of peace, but I teased you that it looked more like a turkey."

Samantha recalled that he had done so one year when their families had gotten together for a Christmas eggnog. She smiled at the memory and unconsciously leaned over to nudge his arm. "You were mean and cruel that year." She took the bird from him and straightened its tail feathers. Then she threw her head back and laughed. "It does look like a turkey!" They laughed into each other's eyes, and Samantha became aware of a warm contentment she couldn't ever remember feeling before. By the look in Brad's eyes, he felt it too.

Then suddenly his smile faded, and he straightened. "I'd better get going. I have to make rounds at the hospital." He started for the front door.

Samantha jumped to her feet. "Brad?" When he turned back to her, she saw that the sternness of recent weeks had returned to his features. "Thank you for helping with the tree. We couldn't have managed without you."

"No problem." He started to turn away again, and she hurried forward.

"Did my father tell you that he's thinking about cutting back on some of his professional duties to spend more time at home?" She smiled. "He's also thinking of coaching Jonathan's baseball team next spring."

"No, he didn't tell me."

"Dad claims that you said some things that started him thinking—about needing people and making time for family." She tried to hold his gaze because he seemed about to turn away again. He'd apologized for not consulting her in his career decision. She owed him an apology too. "He also told me that you made it clear to him—before coming to a formal agreement about the practice—that you had no professional interest in anything beyond the welfare of your patients."

Brad's steely gaze met hers. "I told you that too, Samantha."

"I know. I didn't believe you then. I'm sorry."

"Forget it."

"I . . . guess we both made a few mistakes."

He smiled but without any trace of warmth or mirth. "Yeah, I guess we did. But it doesn't really matter anymore, does it?"

"Doesn't it?"

"No. Look, Samantha, I can't do this any more. It's over, and I've accepted it. Maybe someday we can discuss it all objectively and even laugh about it. But not now. Maybe not for a long time. Now if you'll excuse me, I've got patients waiting for me."

When the door had closed behind him, Samantha walked to the window and watched his car disappear down the road. "I'm sorry, Brad," she murmured, "but I won't give up that easily."

His apology on Thanksgiving Day had removed the last of her reservations about him, and she knew now she would never love anyone but Brad. Had never been *in love* with anyone but him. She'd cared deeply for her husband and had appreciated his dedication to their marriage and their son. But it hadn't been this all-consuming love and passion. And she couldn't believe Brad's love had died so easily either. "We'll talk again, Brad darling. Sooner than you think."

* * *

As he waited for the light to change on the drive to the hospital, Samantha's last remarks filtered back to Brad. So she believed him now and had even apologized. So what? It made little difference in the overall scheme of things. She still needed something he couldn't give her, and he'd accepted that. He wouldn't allow his hopes to rise again.

No, Sam, he thought. *I won't go back to that hell of indecision and inevitable disappointment. The physical attraction might tempt us for a while, but we both know we're better off without each other.*

At least he still had the work he loved, and she'd be happy once she found that eight-to-five guy she wanted so badly. Maybe she'd already found him. Turning into the hospital parking lot, he forced his mind back to the problems of the patients he'd come to see.

Brad checked his watch again as Benton Howard rambled on. Their conversation had begun as a discussion of a particular patient's problem and had evolved into this philosophical discourse on the art of healing. Brad had just shifted uncomfortably for the third time when he heard the front door slam. He stiffened and swore under his breath!

She was home.

He'd been afraid this would happen. He'd successfully avoided her for the past two weeks, but Benton's long-windedness today had done him in. Mumbling that he had to get back to the office, Brad tucked charts and papers into his briefcase and bid Benton a hasty good-bye.

Once out of the study, he looked neither right nor left and made a beeline for the front door. He had almost reached it when a chipper greeting brought him to a halt. "Hi, Brad!"

Brad breathed a sigh of relief and turned. "Hey, Jon." He walked back to the kitchen, where the boy knelt on a chair at the table, pulling papers from an open backpack. At the stove, Josie stirred a pot from which a delicious aroma emanated. Brad nodded to her before turning back to Jonathan. "Was that you I just heard come in the door?"

"Yeah. Hey look, Brad! We're having a Christmas Pageant. You want to come?"

"I don't think I can, Jon."

"But you don't even know when it is." He fumbled through a sheaf of papers and extracted a printed red sheet, holding it out for Brad to see. "It's next Thursday night." He gazed up at Brad with hopeful, pleading eyes. "Craig's mom and dad are coming, and so are Joey's. Maybe you could come with my mom."

Distressed by the child's eager plea, Brad swallowed hard. "I'm going to be busy on Thursday night, Jonathan."

"Then could you at least come to the party afterwards? Maybe you'll be done by then."

"I don't think so."

"What do you have to do?"

"I, uh . . ."

"You never do stuff with us anymore. Can't you come for just a little while? The other guys' dads are coming."

Brad's shoulders slumped in frustration. "Come into the living room, Jon. I want to talk to you."

They sat on the couch, facing each other—Jonathan sitting on his heels. "Look sport," Brad began. "I'm sure your mom will get married again someday, and then you'll have a real dad. And he'll do all kinds of things with you. He'll come to all of your school activities."

"Maybe you'll be him."

The gleam of hopeful anticipation in the boy's eyes tore at Brad. He reached over and squeezed one of Jonathan's knees. "I don't think so, sport."

"Don't you like us anymore?"

Brad pulled the boy close and wrapped an arm around him. "Of course I like you, Jon. You're one of my favorite people in the whole world. I just don't think your mother and I will ever get married. Grown-ups have to have special feelings for each other to do that."

Jon gazed at Brad in silence, and his chin began to quiver. "I want you to be my new dad."

Agony and compassion welled up in Brad's throat. "Aw, Jon, it's more complicated than that."

A tear slipped down Jonathan's cheek and his face crumpled. "Uh-uh! You're just saying that! You don't like us anymore!" He leaped down from the sofa and ran towards his bedroom, almost colliding with Samantha as she came in the front door.

"Jonathan! Are you crying? What's the matter?"

She started to follow him and then saw Brad. And he had to make a conscious effort to harden himself against those wide blue eyes. "Brad," she breathed softly, then looked in the direction her son had disappeared. "Why is Jonathan crying?"

"He asked me to come to his Christmas pageant. Said all of his friend's fathers will be there. He hoped I'd come with you."

She closed her eyes in pain for her son. "Oh, no."

"He's upset and confused about the relationship between the three of us, Samantha. Maybe you'd better try and explain it to him. I just botched the job when I tried."

Her troubled eyes flickered in the direction her son had disappeared. Then she swallowed hard and nodded.

Brad couldn't take his eyes off her. Didn't the woman ever look anything but drop-dead gorgeous? Even after a long day at the office for cripe's sake? He forced his thoughts back to Jonathan. "Tell him I'm sorry. If I thought it was in his best interests, you know I'd come."

Her gaze flickered again towards the bedrooms. "Poor Jonathan. I'll go and talk to him right now." As he met her troubled gaze, Brad felt the wall around his emotions threaten to crumble, and he headed for the door.

Moments later, Samantha hurried to Jonathan's room. She tried to explain the situation to him, but for much of the time, his flat, emotionless gaze shifted from her to the bedspread on which he sat, plucking at the fabric with his fingers. In the end, however, she told herself she'd made him understand.

Samantha arrived home early on the evening of the Christmas pageant. She helped Josie prepare dinner so that they could eat earlier than usual, and when they had things fairly well in hand, she glanced at the clock. The lateness of the hour startled her.

Where was Jonathan? He should have been home long ago. Perhaps he'd slipped into her father's room. Samantha checked, but Dr. Howard had not seen him. At forty minutes past his usual time of arrival, she began to worry and walked out to the front sidewalk in hope of catching a glimpse of him dawdling. But he was nowhere in sight.

When he still had not come home at an hour past his usual time, she became seriously concerned. After one more trip outside to scan the neighborhood, she snatched up her purse and told Josie that she was going to look for him.

Driving towards the school, Samantha's gaze raked the sidewalks and yards along the way in the hope of catching a glimpse of her son but to no avail. When she arrived at the school, the parking lot looked eerily deserted, containing only a few scattered cars. She pulled into a space near the front door and hurried inside.

Reaching Jonathan's classroom, Samantha found the door locked. Then looking frantically around, she saw a beam of light escaping through the doorway of the auditorium and hurried towards it. Inside the cavernous room, Jonathan's teacher and another woman adjusted items on a festively decorated stage. Mrs. Randolph saw Samantha first and turned to greet her. Her smile faded, however, when she saw Samantha's expression.

"Is Jonathan here, Mrs. Randolph? He hasn't come home yet."

The teacher's expression turned concerned. "Why no, Samantha. I sent him home at the usual time."

Samantha struggled to subdue a rising panic. "Where could he be? He should have been home over an hour ago. I searched the neighborhood on the way over here, but there was no sign of him."

Mrs. Randolph put an arm around Samantha's shoulders and steered her out of the auditorium. "Let's go and look in the daycare room. Perhaps he came back for some reason."

But the daycare room was deserted, and as they left it and re-entered the corridor, Mrs. Randolph turned to Samantha with a frown. "Has Jonathan been upset about something lately? Perhaps that might be a clue as to where he's gone."

"I don't think so. Has he seemed upset to you?"

"Actually, yes, he has. He's been acting very distracted for the past week or so. And his work hasn't been up to his usual standards. I thought about calling you, but then decided to wait until after Christmas. I thought he might just be preoccupied with the approaching holidays."

Now that Mrs. Randolph mentioned it, Samantha had noticed that Jonathan spent more time indoors lately—usually watching television. But she hadn't thought his behavior remarkable enough to worry about.

"And he seems more withdrawn with the other children," Mrs. Randolph continued. "He hasn't been participating in games at recess, and today he even asked me if he could stay inside and read. I've been puzzled about it because he's usually one of the first ones out the door."

"I don't know how to explain it, Mrs. Randolph. And I can't think where else to look for him. I don't know what to do." She fought to think clearly. "Maybe he's come home while I've been gone. I'll check back there before doing anything else."

"Yes, that's a good idea, dear. And if he's not at home, you might try calling his friends. Perhaps they could shed some light on where he's gone. He seems to be good friends with Craig Johnson."

Samantha thanked Mrs. Randolph and hurried back to her car. Driving home, she looked for Jonathan again, and as she squinted into the growing darkness, her alarm grew. Her baby was out there somewhere, and the night had turned bitterly cold. Where could he be? *Please, please,* she prayed, *let him be at home when I get there.*

As she arrived at the house and pulled into the driveway, Samantha recognized Brad's car next door. Had it been there when she'd left? She hadn't noticed. Could Jonathan have seen it and gone over to talk to Brad? He had complained several times in the past few weeks that Brad never spent time with them anymore.

Samantha almost tripped in her haste as she bolted out of the car and ran towards the Davis home. She gave only one quick knock before pushing the door open. Mary Davis met her in the foyer.

"Is Jonathan here?" Samantha gasped. Behind Mary, Brad and his father sat together in the living room.

"No, dear, he's not." A frown of concern creased Mary's brow. "Samantha, you're white as a sheet. What's happened?"

Samantha took a deep breath in an effort to stem the rising panic that threatened to burst through her fragile wall of self-control. "He never came home from school today. I can't find him anywhere, and it's dark outside. And freezing cold." Her voice trembled, and she instinctively raised a hand to cover her mouth. "Oh God, where can he be?"

Brad was at her side in an instant. "Did you check at the school? Maybe he had to stay late for some reason?"

"Yes, yes . . . I've looked everywhere."

Then she remembered Mrs. Randolph's last admonition. "Mrs. Randolph suggested I call Craig." She turned to leave. "I have his number at home."

"I'll go with you." Brad reached for his coat, which hung on a rack near the door.

As they entered the Howard house, Benton and Josie met them in the foyer, also looking anxious and pale. "Is he here?" Samantha gasped, but the expressions on their faces answered her question.

Racing to the kitchen, she fumbled through the telephone book. When she tried to dial Craig's number, her fingers shook so badly that Brad had to finish dialing for her.

"Jon was crying after school today, Mrs. Richards," Craig told her. "When I asked him what was wrong, he said his dad couldn't come to the pageant tonight."

Samantha's gaze flew to Brad's. "His dad?"

"Yeah, the guy that's going to be his new dad. You know, Brad."

All she could do was stare at Brad, feeling a sudden wave of light-headedness.

He took the phone from her. "Craig? Will you repeat what you just told Mrs. Richards?"

Now Brad's gaze flew to Samantha's and locked there. He looked as though the wind had been knocked out of him. "Did he say anything else, Craig? Do you have any idea where he might have gone?" He listened for a moment. "Okay, thanks. Please call us if you hear from him." Brad hung up the telephone.

"What did he say? Does he have any idea where Jonathan might be?" Dr. Howard's voice was tight with anxiety.

"He said Jonathan seemed upset because I wouldn't come to the pageant tonight."

"What? Oh, that can't be what this is all about."

"Maybe it can." Brad turned to Samantha. "I'll go out and search the neighborhood for him again. I'll stop back at the school."

She pulled her coat around herself. "I'll go with you."

Brad put his hands on her shoulders. "Maybe you should stay here in case he comes home, Sam." He looked from Dr. Howard to Josie to Samantha. "And if I'm not back in half an hour, I think you'd better call the police."

Samantha sucked in a sharp breath but held her emotions in check—just barely. She followed Brad to the front door, and stood just outside, watching him as he ran towards his car. *Please, please,* she prayed, *let him find Jonathan.*

Brad paused before getting into his car. "Go back inside, Sam. It's freezing out here." Numbly, she turned to obey. She'd just stepped into the house, when Brad's voice rang out again.

"Samantha!"

The note of urgency brought her rushing outside once more. Brad was leaning into his car, and when he straightened, he held something in his arms. "He's here!"

Samantha stumbled down the stairs. Soaring hope and agonizing fear churned sickeningly inside her. *Oh God, please let him be all right.* Then she heard his voice.

"Brad?" The child sounded dazed.

"You okay, sport?"

A moan escaped his lips. "I'm cold." Samantha heard his teeth chatter.

The next moment, her son was in her arms. "Oh,

Jonathan, Jonathan. Where have you been? We were so worried."

Brad whipped his own coat off and wrapped it around the boy. Then his arm came around Samantha, and he ushered them both towards the house.

Dr. Howard and Josie met them at the door. Once inside, Brad took Jon from his mother and carried him into the living room, where a fire burned in the fireplace. He pulled off the large coat, and setting Jonathan close to the fire, rubbed his arms and legs briskly. Then he turned to Josie and asked her to get Jonathan a hot drink.

When Jon had stopped shivering and sat sipping his hot chocolate, Samantha sat next to him on the sofa. "Jonathan, why didn't you come home after school? Where have you been all this time?"

He looked down into his cup. "I just walked around. I don't want to go to the pageant tonight."

"Why not, sweetheart? What's happened?" Samantha hugged him to herself.

Jonathan glanced at Brad and then into his cup of chocolate again. "I told everybody Brad was coming, but he's not." His chin began to tremble. "I told 'em that maybe he was gonna be my new dad." The last was spoken barely above a whisper. Tears brimmed and spilled down his cheeks. "Now they'll think I lied. But I really thought that maybe . . ." His voice choked, and his little body began to shake with sobs.

"Oh, honey." Samantha took his cup from him and setting it aside, lifted him onto her lap, rocking him gently. "But why did you get into Brad's car?"

"I got cold," he sobbed. "And I thought if Brad came out, I could ask him again to come."

Brad squatted down in front of the boy. "You know

what, Jon? I'm not busy tonight after all. If you still want me to come to the pageant, I will."

Jonathan hiccuped and wiped at his cheeks with both hands. "You will?"

"Sure. You bet. Because we're good friends."

Jonathan thought about that for a moment and then slowly nodded his head. "Okay."

Then Benton Howard propelled himself forward on his crutches. "And you know what else, Jon? With Brad along to help, I'll bet I can manage to come too." He patted a crutch with one hand. "I'm getting pretty good on these things."

A hesitant smile curled Jonathan's lips. "Really, Grampa?" His gaze moved between his grandfather and Brad. "You'll both come?"

"Absolutely," his grandfather assured him.

Samantha rose, giving Jonathan a gentle nudge from her lap. "We'd better hurry, or we'll be late."

Brad called his parents to tell them Jonathan was all right, and less than an hour later, they arrived at the school. Samantha rushed her son backstage while Brad found seats and got Dr. Howard settled. Then, just as the production started, Samantha slipped into her seat, between the two men.

When her churning emotions began to settle, Samantha became very aware of the men sitting on either side of her. It felt so right to be here with both of them. She glanced at her father, who chuckled as Jonathan entered the stage, wearing a shepherd's costume and holding the cane that Dr. Howard had brought back from Scotland the year before.

Samantha leaned back in her seat and turned her head enough so that she could observe Brad on her other side. His mouth too was curved in a smile—

albeit a wistful one. She suddenly wanted to slip her arm through his as they watched Jon together. He'd been so gentle with her son tonight when he'd offered to come to the play.

Feelings of gratitude and affection flooded her. Then as she snatched another glimpse of him, her emotions brimmed. No, not affection. Love. She was desperately in love with this man as she had been for most of her life.

But would Brad ever learn to love her again? Could tonight possibly become a turning point? The familiar scent of his aftershave drifted to her nostrils and an intense physical awareness moved through her. The effort to resist reaching out to him became almost painful.

Then his elbow moved on the armrest between them, nudging hers. He glanced at her and after a moment, removed his arm. The aloofness had returned to his manner. After that, his eyes remained riveted on the stage.

At the party after the pageant, Jonathan proudly introduced his family and Brad to his friends. When one little boy innocently asked whether Brad would soon become Jonathan's new father, Jon bravely told him that right now, they were just good friends.

Watching them, Samantha's heart came close to breaking. If Brad never became a part of their family, a good portion of the blame rested with her. She'd misjudged Brad and in the process, let her son down in this most important of ways.

Then she noticed Mrs. Randolph walking in their direction. Samantha had rushed Jonathan into the auditorium, just as the play was about to start, and hadn't had a chance to explain his reappearance to his teacher. Now Samantha explained the situation in the most tactful terms she could manage.

Mrs. Randolph's gaze skimmed them all and she smiled. "Thank goodness it all turned out all right."

Brad nodded and tried to smile, but his nerves were on edge. Sitting next to Samantha during the play and standing with her now, trying to make casual conversation, was wearing on him. He had to keep reminding himself that she was off limits because his entire being gravitated towards her. When she'd been so upset over Jonathan's disappearance, he'd wanted to take her into his arms.

Just then Annie's mother—the woman he'd met at Jonathan's open house—caught his eye from across the room and gave him a flirtatious smile. Brad gave a stiff smile back and nodded half-heartedly. She was an attractive woman, but next to Samantha's fresh beauty, hers seemed artificial and lusterless. But then in his eyes, all beauty dimmed next to Samantha's. His gaze moved helplessly back to her, and he saw that she'd been watching him. He looked away again, telling himself that he had to stop this. Had to wean himself from this obsession with her.

He also had to wean Jonathan's affections from himself. How had the boy become so attached to him? He hadn't realized just how attached until the episode tonight. It scared him, and he knew that he'd have to treat Jon gently for a while. Hopefully, when Jon formed stronger friendships with his peers, Brad would become less important to him. And if this other man worked out for Samantha, all the better. He swallowed the sick feeling that welled into his throat at that last thought.

Chapter Ten

Over the next few days, Samantha forced herself to think about plans for Christmas. They would have a quiet celebration this year—just the three of them. But she told herself that their improved relationship would make the occasion especially happy.

She'd been trying unsuccessfully to put Brad out of her mind—especially since the night of the pageant. He had almost totally ignored her once they'd found Jonathan. And afterwards, when he'd brought them home, he'd come inside only long enough to get her father settled. He'd hardly looked her way when he said good-night. Perhaps she would have to get used to the fact that he no longer cared for her after all. Would have to stop nurturing futile hopes.

Then one afternoon, a few days after the pageant, Mary Davis called and, to Samantha's surprise, invited them all to Christmas dinner. "Cindy and Bob and the children are coming," she told Samantha. "I thought the boys would enjoy playing together, and we adults can have a nice long visit. We see each other too seldom these days."

"How nice of you to ask us," Samantha exclaimed, her spirits rising. "I'll speak to Dad, but I'm sure he'll agree wholeheartedly. And Jonathan will be so excited."

"You did what?" Brad's eyebrows shot upward. "Mom, didn't it ever occur to you that Samantha and I might be uncomfortable in each other's presence for an entire day?"

"Samantha didn't sound concerned. In fact, she sounded very happy that we'd invited them." Mary Davis gave her son a sidelong glance. "Besides, we can use all the holiday cheer we can get around here. Heaven knows you haven't contributed much of it to our gatherings lately."

"What do you mean? I'm cheerful enough."

"Oh, Brad, you've been in a black funk for weeks. And you refuse to tell any of us what's bothering you."

"Nothing's bothering me," he growled.

"Uh-huh. Well, if this is a permanent condition with you, then we can definitely use a few more happy faces around here on Christmas Day."

"Maybe I should just stay away then. Let everyone enjoy the day without my brooding presence."

Mary slapped her paring knife down on the kitchen counter and shook a half-peeled potato at her son. "Bradley Christopher Davis, if you're more than ten minutes late on Christmas Day, I swear I'll send your father and Bob out to drag you here bodily. Don't you even think of ruining the holiday for the rest of the family."

Brad breathed an irritated sigh and reached for a piece of raw potato, popping it into his mouth. "All right, all right. I'll be here. Geez, talk about being treated like a kid."

Mary smiled mischievously as her son exited the house, closing the door behind himself with unnecessary gusto.

Christmas Day arrived cold, crisp, and clear. And Brad appeared at the family home not only on time but early. Since he had no emergencies that morning, he came to watch the children unwrap their presents. In addition, he'd gotten one of the residents without family nearby to cover for him in the afternoon. He told himself he didn't want his father and brother-in-law creating a scene at the hospital.

From the moment he'd awakened that morning, his mood felt lighter than it had in weeks. Black funk, huh? He'd show them all how cheerful he could be. He rough-housed with Trevor and even helped baby Elizabeth redress her doll—twice—after she'd pulled off all its clothes.

But as the time drew near for their neighbors to arrive, Brad grew agitated. When the doorbell rang, his entire body tensed as Cindy rose to answer it. He stood as their guests entered but hung back during the hugs of greeting. Finally he stepped forward to shake Benton's hand, squeeze Jon's shoulder, and nod a hello to Samantha.

During the subsequent conversation, he was careful to keep his gaze from Samantha. After a time, however, it willfully drifted her way. She wore a forest-green dress that ended an inch or two above her knees and a red-, green-, and cream-colored silk scarf, casually draped and tied around her shoulders. She looked festive and smart, and Brad's gaze dropped helplessly over her, taking in her slender figure and long shapely legs.

God help him, his emotions came alive at the sight of her. Reining them in, he turned to join the discussion between his father and Benton.

Soon the women drifted off to examine several of the tree ornaments and other holiday decorations in the house, and when they moved into the kitchen to check on dinner, the rest of the party settled down to watch televised football.

But the game didn't hold Brad's interest. His gaze kept drifting to the door of the kitchen. He'd almost given in to an urge to check out the progress of dinner himself, when Trevor and Jonathan brought a game to him that Trevor had gotten for Christmas. "Uncle Brad, will you help us read the instructions and show us how to play?"

"I'm watching the game, Trevor." Brad's gaze distractedly flickered again towards the kitchen door.

"Please, Uncle Brad? Just read the directions to us once, and we'll play by ourselves."

Brad stifled a groan and reached for the sheet of paper that Trevor held out to him. "You need four people to play this game," he told his nephew.

"If we find somebody else, will you play with us? Mommy says it's a short game."

Brad only half listened. "Yeah, yeah, okay."

Trevor turned to his father. "Dad, will you play with us?"

"I'm busy, son." He gave a yelp of enthusiasm at the Detroit Lions' interception.

"Grampa, will you play with us?" But all four of the men ignored the boys now, cheering as the Lions scored a touchdown.

Just then Samantha wandered into the living room. "Mom, will you play this game with us? We need one more person."

Samantha took the box from Jonathan. "Oh, I remember this one." She smiled. "I guess we have time for a quick game before dinner, but we need one more player."

"Uncle Brad said he'd play." Samantha and Brad's gazes collided. Hurriedly the boys set up the board, and the trapped adults settled themselves on the floor to play.

As Samantha drew her legs up to one side, her skirt retreated to several inches above her knees, despite her efforts to pull it down. When she looked up, she saw that Brad had noticed, and his gaze held hers for a brief moment. Something flickered in his eyes before he looked away.

They began the game, and after some initial guidance, the boys played adeptly and with enthusiasm. Several times as they leapt in glee when one or the other of them gained an advantage, Samantha and Brad exchanged smiles. And once, as their eyes met, Brad also gave Samantha a conspiratorial wink—which rattled her composure. They had just finished the game when Mrs. Davis announced the turkey was ready for carving.

Soon they all moved into the dining room, and Samantha felt her cheeks grow warm as she noticed that Brad's place card stood above the plate next to her own. She glanced at him and saw him narrow his eyes at his mother and shake his head. Following their prayer of thanks, choruses of ooh's and aah's echoed along the table as they passed around the various dishes.

Samantha hardly tasted her meal because her stomach contracted each time Brad's arm brushed hers or when their elbows bumped. But the board game had relieved some of the tension between them, and they laughed at their mutual clumsiness. As the meal wore on, they even began to talk about friends they had in common and interesting developments at the hospital.

When they had finished dessert and the adults sat around the table sipping coffee, Elizabeth came in from the living room where the children had gone to play. She tugged on Brad's arm. "Unca Brad, put on baby's shoes."

Brad took the doll from her. "I've helped you dress her twice already. Why do you keep taking her clothes off?" But he set the doll in his lap and his big fingers fumbled to insert the tiny foot into the first shoe. Then in taking the second shoe from Elizabeth, his gaze brushed Samantha's as she watched him, smiling. He shoved the second foot into its shoe and handed the doll back to Elizabeth, his gaze meeting Samantha's once more. A playful grin spread over his face, and he shrugged. "Hey, I'm a sensitive guy."

Samantha couldn't help laughing out loud, and the other adults joined her, proceeding to tease Brad about his newfound skill. But Samantha couldn't bring herself to tease him. His gentleness with Elizabeth had touched a spot deep within her. Finally admonishing the others to stop embarrassing him, she reached over without thinking to caress his arm. As she did so, she felt his whole body quake, and his gaze flew to hers. She snatched her hand away and felt her cheeks flush again.

Then the boisterous little boys entered the room, waving a sprig of mistletoe. Trevor stood on tiptoe, and holding it over his mother's head, urged his father to kiss her. When Bob willingly complied, Trevor moved on to hold it over his grandmother. Both boys laughed with glee as the Davises also kissed. Then Trevor moved to Samantha. "Dr. Howard and Uncle Brad both have to kiss Samantha," he insisted. Benton Howard—on Samantha's other side—leaned over to place a light kiss on his daughter's cheek.

As Brad followed suit, a chorus of nay-saying rang out. Benton was Samantha's father, but Brad couldn't get away with such a little peck. Heat scorched Samantha's cheeks. Then she felt Brad's arm extend across the back of her chair, and when she looked up at him, she wasn't sure whether she felt relief or further embarrassment at his leer of mock flirtation.

"Pucker up, Samantha," he admonished as his mouth moved towards hers. Their lips touched briefly, and when Brad pulled back, the look on his face bordered on alarm. He stared at her dazedly for a few seconds before turning away and forcing a smile. He uttered something, which produced a chorus of laughter, but Samantha's heart beat so loudly, she didn't hear it.

When the conversation had drifted back to general topics, Samantha began gathering dishes from the table. She needed to get out of the room to regain her composure. Mary started to collect a few too, but then became engrossed in a conversation with Cindy and

Bob and sat down again. Brad took the plates from his mother and followed Samantha to the kitchen.

He entered to the sight of her gazing out the window at the large snowflakes that had begun to fall.

"Look," she murmured. "Isn't it beautiful. A white Christmas."

He moved closer. He could smell her hair, and he had to clench his fists to keep from touching her. "Beautiful," he whispered, but he wasn't looking at the snow. He experienced the familiar sense of wonder at her flawless beauty. When she turned to smile at him, his eyes dropped to her lips and their moist softness entranced and pulled at him. He became vaguely aware that the distance between them was closing.

Riiiiiing! The loud jangle of the kitchen telephone ripped the air.

Brad snapped upright. Then giving his head a single shake to clear it, he reached for the telephone. "Davis residence." When he heard the voice at the other end of the line, he threw a quick glance Samantha's way, then turned to the telephone. "Yeah, Greg?" He had to force himself to concentrate on what the resident was saying. "You can't handle it? Is she hemorrhaging badly?" He nodded then and turned to face Samantha, his gaze holding hers with a degree of challenge. "I'll be right there, Greg."

He hung up the phone, and his tone turned brusque. "Problems with one of our patients. I have to get to the hospital."

"I heard." When he turned to leave, she added, "It's nice that you've had the whole day."

Brad stopped and faced her again. "Greg's been covering for me, but this is a little over his head."

She nodded. "I understand."

He stared at her, surprised and then puzzled, and the defensiveness he'd felt just moments ago seeped away. When he went back into the dining room, she followed.

Apparently having heard the telephone, Benton Howard directed a questioning look at Brad.

"Helen Baker," Brad told him. "She's hemorrhaging badly. The resident needs help." Brad pulled on his tweed sport jacket and then moved to the closet for his overcoat. Shrugging into it, he turned back to the room. "I'm not sure if I'll be back tonight." He raised a hand in farewell. "Merry Christmas, everybody." His gaze rested on Samantha for a moment before he went out the door.

She moved to the window and watched as he brushed the fluffy snow from his windshield. Then she felt a movement against her leg and looked down to see that Jonathan had come to the window too. He waved wistfully as Brad's car pulled away.

Samantha carried her small suitcase out to the foyer. She didn't feel like going on this ski trip but had committed to it over a month ago. Right now, she just wanted to spend the New Year's weekend with her father and Jonathan—and with her waning hopes that Brad might call or stop by the house when she was at home.

She'd thought about him constantly all week. Being with him on Christmas Day had intensified her longing for him so that she could barely function. She kept remembering their brief kiss under the mistletoe and the stunned way in which he'd looked at her afterwards. She'd thought surely he'd felt something. Their near-kiss in the kitchen had raised her hopes that he might try to see her again.

But obviously he'd only been going along with the festivities, and any warming in his attitude had been in her imagination. Because her father had told her that he'd stopped by mid-afternoon yesterday—when he'd known she was at work. She could only conclude that nothing between them had changed.

How could he have felt nothing when she had felt so much?

The doorbell rang, and Samantha answered it, greeting Ben with forced enthusiasm.

Brad pulled up to the Howard house and swore under his breath: Two cars stood in the driveway, Samantha's and that blasted red sports car. So she was still seeing ol' Ben, was she?

Then Brad had been right to stay away. His reason had battled with his inclinations all week. Several times he'd almost called her or stopped in at Dwyer's office. But whenever he'd come close to weakening, he'd reminded himself that she needed something he could never give her. Nothing significant had changed since they'd both come to that conclusion weeks ago— soft and sweet as she'd seemed on Christmas Day. He paused for a moment, remembering their near and actual kisses. God, she could get him going again so easily.

Best to just avoid her. He should leave now. Come back later.

Then with a growl of annoyance at himself, he bolted from the car. He didn't have time for immature games. He'd greet them both briefly and get on to a discussion of business with Benton.

Brad rang the bell. When no one answered, he knocked and then walked in. No one seemed to be about. "Hello!" he called, but only silence greeted him. Crossing the foyer, he paused to look into the kitchen and found it empty. He had turned to head for Benton's study when the door to the garage opened and Samantha entered, carrying a ski boot in each hand.

"Brad!" The smile she gave him and the sparkle in her eyes sent his emotions churning. "I didn't know you were here."

Then Ben appeared behind her, toting a pair of skis, and every muscle in Brad's body tensed. He eyed them both. "Going skiing?"

Samantha nodded, her smile slipping a bit. "Boyne Mountain."

Together? he wanted to ask, but his pride wouldn't let him. "I need to talk to your father. I'll just go on back if it's okay." His words came out more clipped than he'd intended.

"Alright. Sure."

He made a move towards Benton's room but couldn't pull his gaze from Samantha's. Her eyes looked troubled.

"Hope you get some free time this weekend."

He nodded. "Yeah, me too."

He started to turn away again, but she stepped towards him. "Dad said after the first of the year, he may start coming into the office for a couple of hours each day. That'll give you some relief."

"That's good to hear."

Her long blond hair was tied back in a ponytail, her cheeks flushed pink. She looked young and vulnerable, and his predictable libido stirred. But he couldn't just stand here, staring at her. He took a couple of steps backward. "Is uh, your father in his bedroom or the study?"

"The study."

He nodded and tried to smile. "Happy New Year."

"Happy New Year, Brad."

Something in her voice pulled at him, but he finally managed to turn away. As he headed for the back of the house, an emptiness filled him, then anger gripped his belly when he passed the small suitcase in the foyer. Gritting his teeth, he looked up to see Jonathan coming down the hallway towards him. "Hi Jon. How's it going?"

Jonathan shrugged, looking glum. "Okay."

Brad glanced again at the suitcase. "Are you going skiing too?"

He shook his head. "Uh-uh, only Mom. She's gonna be gone the whole weekend."

With Ben? he wanted to ask, but again he didn't. He tamped down the unreasonable anger that burned inside. "Let's go talk to your Grandpa. Maybe the three of us guys can manage to stay awake until midnight on New Year's Eve." Jonathan nodded and followed on Brad's heels.

Benton Howard looked up from his desk when Brad entered. "I was hoping you'd stop by. How did Betty Potter's bowel resection go this morning?"

Brad let himself fall heavily into a chair on the opposite side of the desk. "As well as could be expected. She *is* seventy-nine years old."

"Nothing you couldn't handle though, I expect." Brad described the procedure and the woman's present stable condition. Nodding, Dr. Howard closed another patient's chart he'd been perusing. "Looks like Jim

Donaldson's doing well. You did good work on him too."

Then his gaze strayed towards the door of the room. "Is Samantha about ready to leave? They ought to get started. There's a forecast for heavy snow later tonight."

"They?" So she *was* going with him. Brad's throat went dry.

"Yes, she and Ben." Benton smiled conspiratorially. "They must be getting pretty serious if she's going away with him for the weekend."

Brad's fingers tightened over the arms of the chair. He fought to keep his face expressionless, but knew he was glaring at Benton Howard, irritated by the man's matter-of-fact tone.

Just then, a knock sounded at the door and Samantha entered. "We're leaving, Dad."

"Good, good. Hope you make it all the way there before the snow starts."

Samantha crossed the room to plant a kiss on his forehead. Then she turned to her son, who was playing with a truck on the floor. He hadn't looked up since her entrance. "Can I have a good-bye hug, Jonathan?"

He rose and came to her but gave her only a brief, perfunctory embrace before pulling away.

A worried look crossed her brow. "We'll do something fun next weekend, okay?"

"Okay." But his tone was expressionless, and he'd already returned to his truck.

Then she looked up at Brad. And for the brief moment their gazes held, he thought he saw a longing in her eyes. But after a sedate good-bye, she left, closing the door behind her.

A sudden jab of agitation shot Brad to his feet, and

he paced the floor as Benton proceeded to discuss another patient's problem. Unhearing and with his emotions seething, Brad interrupted the older man mid-sentence. "This whole thing doesn't bother you?"

"What?" Dr. Howard glanced at the patient's record in his hand with a confused look.

"Samantha, for cripe's sake!"

"What about her?"

"It doesn't bother you that she's going off for the whole weekend with that . . . that . . . Ben!"

Howard's smile reflected good-humored tolerance. "Samantha's an adult and a level-headed one. She can take care of herself." He returned doggedly to the subject of their patient.

Brad dropped back into the chair, making little effort to listen to his partner's discourse. His insides churned. How the devil would he get through the weekend, knowing she was with another man? Should he have tried to stop her? Those looks she'd given him—did she still feel something?

He felt a tug on his leg and opened his arms to Jonathan, who climbed into his lap. "I wish Mom was staying here with us for New Year's."

"So do I, Jon. So do I."

Then his gaze collided with Benton Howard's. A challenge gleamed in the older man's eyes. *So what are you going to do about it?*

Brad frowned, then stood and lowered Jonathan to the floor. "Stay here with your grandfather, Jon." He pulled open the door and hurried towards the front of the house.

"Samantha?" he called. But only silence greeted him. Then he heard a car start outside.

"Samantha!" Panic gripped him, and he dashed out the front door, calling her name again, loudly.

She paused in getting into the car.

Brad sucked in the fresh, cool air in an effort to calm himself. "Can I talk to you for a minute, Samantha?"

"We're in a hurry to get on the road, Brad."

He started down the porch steps. "It's important."

She studied his expression, then turned and said something to Ben. Closing the car door, she came towards him. "What is it?"

He took her arm. "Inside."

When they'd closed the front door behind them, Brad faced her and drew a shaky breath. "Please, don't go away with Ben, Samantha."

She looked surprised, and then her eyes brightened. "You don't want me to go?"

He shook his head. Then running a shaky hand through his hair, he paced the foyer before coming to stand in front of her again. "If I go with the medical group . . . will you consider a future between us? Could you handle that kind of life? I'll give up the practice with your father."

She stared at him. Her mouth opened but no words came.

"I can't stand the thought of you with another man, Samantha," Brad hurried on. "I'm in love with you. I need you, and I want to marry you. I can't live without you anymore."

Her eyes filled with tears. "But you love the work you do with my father."

His jaw tightened. His throat moved in a deep swallow. "I love you more."

Joy surged inside her, but she tamped it down. She

wanted him, but not if false pretenses had precipitated this. "I think you should know that Ben and I are just friends. We're going up to Boyne with a group. Meeting the others there. I'm rooming with his sister."

She saw relief in his eyes, and he expelled a ragged breath. But he also squared his shoulders in determination. "I still don't want you to go. I want you here with me. With us."

Their gazes held, and she smiled. "Okay." She shrugged. "I didn't really want to go anyway."

That familiar smile stole across his face—the one she'd loved all her life. He stepped towards her, took her head in his hands, and lowered his face to hers. "I love you, Samantha Jane," he rumbled. "I think I've always loved you."

Her arms slid around his waist, and she looked into those eyes that took her breath away. "I loved you first. Even when you thought I was a little pest."

"I never thought you were a pest."

She laughed. "Liar."

He grinned. "You were always so darn cute. How could I object to a good-looking female following me around?" Then his smile faded, and an intensity grew in his eyes. Slowly he lowered his mouth to hers. He tugged on the band that held her hair. And when the blond mist cascaded around her shoulders, he pushed his hands and then his face into it. He kissed her eyes, her nose, her neck. "Oh God, Samantha," he breathed. "I love you. Don't ever leave me."

She nuzzled his neck, inhaled his familiar scent. "Never," she whispered. "I can't live without you anymore either." They clung to each other.

The toot of a horn outside brought them back to

reality. Samantha pulled back to look into his eyes. "I'd better tell Ben."

Brad released her reluctantly. "I'll give you a few minutes, then come out and help you bring in your things."

She nodded and hurried outside.

When Brad followed minutes later, she had pulled the small suitcase out of the back of the car. Ben, meanwhile, was releasing her skis from the outer rack.

To Brad's surprise, the other man didn't seem upset. When Brad reached out to take the skis from him, he smiled. "It's about time you two realized this was inevitable."

They shook hands. "Thanks for understanding."

Turning to Samantha, Ben added, "You're missing some good snow, but maybe another time we can talk you both into joining us." With a quick wave, he slipped into the seat of his sleek car and headed towards the highway.

They carried her luggage and ski gear back into the house. Setting everything down in the foyer, they faced each other again. Brad straightened and pushing his sport coat aside, rested his hands at his waist with an air of resigned determination. "I'd better go in and talk to your father. I'm sure he won't have any trouble finding someone else to take my place." He tried to smile, but behind it, she saw the pain.

She reached up to touch his face. "Brad, darling. How can I ask you to leave my father's practice when I know how much you love it?"

He took her hand, kissed her palm. "It's okay, sweetheart. We made a deal."

She slid her arms inside his coat and around his middle. "I don't recall agreeing to it."

"It's all right, Samantha. I can endure anything as long as I have you."

She nestled closer until his arms encircled her too. "I couldn't love you and watch you *endure* one situation when you absolutely *revel* in another."

Samantha raised herself to place a light kiss on his lips. "It took me a while to learn to trust you, Brad, but I *have* learned. I know now that you'll always spend as much time with us and with our family as you possibly can.

"Besides," she tossed her head. "I'm going to be rather busy myself for the next several years. First having more babies, of course. And once they're all in school, I just might take some classes myself. Maybe become a nurse practitioner."

He looked into her eyes. "Are you sure about this? About my staying on with your father?"

"Positive."

"Samantha? Brad? What's taking so long out there?"

They looked at each other with dancing eyes; then Brad grinned. "He tricked me, you know. He told me that you and Ben were getting serious."

Samantha laughed. "Ah well, trickery's better than the proverbial shotgun fathers used to use to avenge a daughter's honor." She pushed her face up close to his. "Because you did compromise me, you know. You made me fall in love with you when I was little more than a child."

"Does that mean you'll marry me?"

"Try and get rid of me."

"Hey! Will somebody come in here and tell us what's going on?"

"Mom? Can I come out now?"

They kissed once more and Brad smiled down at her.

"Shall we go in and tell them?"

"Jonathan will be thrilled, you know."

"That makes two of us."

"Three," she murmured.

"Samantha! Brad!" a deep voice boomed out louder than ever. They smiled into each other's eyes. "Four," they said in unison.

Hand in hand, they walked to Benton Howard's study.